Praise for *Unsafe Words*:

"With *Unsafe Words*, Loren Rhoads has created a lyrical kaleidoscope of a collection, whose shifting genres reveal ever-evolving visions of shining beauty and immense darkness. I loved it."

— Brian Hodge, author of *The Immaculate Void* and
Skidding Into Oblivion

"Loren Rhoads is an uncommon writer in any genre. She sharpens tropes to an unrecognizable edge and uses them to wound you. She raises you from the dead with her unflinching hope and her vital prose. She's the writer you want to hold your hand on the long, strange walk into hell."

— Meg Elison, author of the *Road to Nowhere* series

"*Unsafe Words* is filled with dark, lyrical tales that lift you up before they drag you under into quiet moments of fear and horror. Rhoads has a gift. She takes you deep, and when you come out on the other side, you're just glad you're still alive."

— J. Scott Coatsworth, Captain Awesome of Queer Sci Fi

"Loren Rhoads's work is at once arresting, haunting, unsettling, and gorgeous. Her stories are all the darker for being deeply human and more profoundly human in their darkness."

— Thomas S. Roche, author of *Dark Matter*

"If you're already familiar with Loren's work, you know that you're in for an evocative, rich mélange. If you're just now discovering her...prepare yourself and dig in. Leave your preconceptions and expectations right here, and step boldly into Loren's incredible, beautiful world. Just don't be surprised if your own world looks a little different when you get back."

— Lisa Morton, in her introduction

Unsafe Words

Stories by Loren Rhoads

Automatism Press
San Francisco

Stories and commentary: Loren Rhoads
Introduction: Lisa Morton
Cover art © 2020 by Lynne Hansen (LynneHansenArt.com)
Interior design: Automatism Press

ISBN 978-1-7351876-0-0
ISBN (ebook) 978-1-7351876-1-7

Library of Congress Control Number: 2020916293

Printed in the United States of America.

Check out author readings and other events at https://lorenrhoads.com/

Join Loren's monthly newsletter for behind-the-scenes glimpses and morbid travel essays here: https://mailchi.mp/aa9545b2ccf4/lorenrhoads

Automatism Press
PO Box 12308
San Francisco, CA 94112 USA
www.automatismpress.com

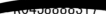

Table of Contents

Introduction

Lisa Morton

I want to live in Loren Rhoads's world.

I don't mean the everyday world of the author herself, although I suspect that's pretty intriguing, too: Loren lives in the heart of one of the world's great cities (San Francisco), edited the brilliant magazine (and resulting book) *Morbid Curiosity*, is a world-class expert on cemeteries, and is a gifted author who (like, I suspect, many other women—we are, after all, schooled from birth to be modest and stand back demurely while the men stride vigorously forward) probably doesn't realize either how good she is or how much she's respected by her peers.

The world I'm talking about is that created by Loren's extraordinary fiction. I think I first read Loren's short stories in a 2008 anthology called *Sins of the Sirens* that gathered together the work of four women horror authors. This was a time (and it's surprising now to realize that it wasn't even that long ago) when women writing horror was something that was still unusual enough to merit extra attention. I'd already read the other three writers in that book, but there was something special about Loren Rhoads, an elegance and a sensuality that, over the years of following her work, I learned to recognize instantly.

I could absolutely pick out a Loren Rhoads story without ever needing to see her name.

It isn't just her remarkable settings and descriptions, or the lush emotions her characters experience, though; it's also the way she uses women in her stories. Loren's women may be put through tense and even horrific situations (how about discovering that you're being stalked by an ageless entity in an isolated location or realizing that the woman you just got intimate with takes photographs of dead things?), but they are never victims. If things go badly for them, they find alternate solutions; they do it naturally, with a resolution and strength that is too seldom recognized in genre fiction.

Loren also has a remarkable touch (no pun intended) with erotic scenes. Her characters—almost all women, nonbinary individuals, or gay men—actually *enjoy* sex; in her horror stories, sex does not automatically lead to death, a formula that was worn out thirty years ago and yet doggedly continues to appear in horror. She's an honest enough writer to admit that sex isn't always good (see the excruciating non-genre story "Sound of Impact") or to have characters take precautions (the moment in "Valentine" when Simon dons a condom), but her protagonists approach sex as a life experience and revel in it when it's good. She takes a refreshingly similar approach to drugs, neither condemning nor promoting their use. The (too often trite) moralizing found in other genre tales will never appear in a Loren Rhoads story.

Music also plays a major part in Loren's fiction, but she never resorts to just quoting lyrics as a shortcut to establish mood; she's more interested in the rhythms and emotional resonances of music. Several of the stories here feature musicians ("The Acid That Dissolves Images," "Never Bargained for You," "Mothflame"); in two of those stories, the musicians aren't entirely human. Loren understands the spell that our musical icons cast upon us, how that particular form of idolatry orbits the way musicians involve our senses to an extent that can consume us, even as we love the consumption.

What you won't find in this book are any of the usual genre tropes. There are no bloodsucking vampires or flesh-hungry zombies here; granted, there are time travelers and aliens in the science fiction stories, but even those are in service of very human themes of love and prejudice. I frankly hope that Loren tries a hardboiled, noir-ish mystery at some point, because I can imagine her distinctive prose serving—and expanding—that genre well.

While I know that the mix of genres in this collection—which includes horror, science fiction, fantasy, fairy tale, and two wrenching stories with virtually no genre elements at all—might make it less appealing to readers who prefer one type of genre over another, I find it refreshing to see an artist at work who is less interested in making her fiction conform to genre than in making genres conform to her own brand of fiction.

If you're already familiar with Loren's work, you know that you're in for an evocative, rich mélange. If you're just now discovering her...prepare yourself and dig in. Leave your preconceptions and expectations right here, and step boldly into Loren's incredible, beautiful world. Just don't be surprised if your own world looks a little different when you get back.

Here There Be Monsters

"You're gonna love this place," Caleb promised. He pulled his bike over to the side of the pot-holed driveway, so Violet stopped, too. The house ahead of them was clearly vacant, its creamy paint gone scabrous as the stucco beneath it had fallen away. The windows—blank, like eyes blinded by cataracts—reflected the flawless cerulean sky overhead. In front of the house stretched a lawn gone to meadow. Its tall golden weeds drowsed in the sun.

Violet and Caleb rounded the lawn—was it heart-shaped?—and went to sit on the broken steps leading up to the veranda. Caleb shouldered out of his backpack and pulled out two sandwiches. They were dill Havarti on sourdough with some lettuce and just a little mustard. Violet smiled, pleased that he'd finally remembered she was vegetarian. After the bike ride up the mountain, the sandwich was perfect, washed down with water from her thermos.

The area around the derelict house seemed eerily quiet. The fall of a leaf, rattling on its way to the ground, echoed. Violet turned so she didn't have her back to the house.

"Wanna go in?" Caleb asked.

"It's too nice a day to go into a haunted house."

He didn't disagree.

When they'd finished their sandwiches, Caleb drew an Altoids box from the back pocket of his jeans. Violet expected a joint, but instead he tipped out two tiny squares of paper.

"Sweets for the sweet," he said, offering her one.

Violet wished he'd said something more serious to honor the sacrament, but took the tab from his palm and popped it into her mouth anyway. The paper left no discernible flavor on her tongue.

Then they retrieved their bikes and walked them back down

around the lawn. The pot-holed driveway they'd been following branched. Faced with the choice, Violet voted for the dirt path heading downward.

Gullies ran through the rich chestnut-colored dirt. Caleb rode his bike over them, making it hop when one gap crossed the path diagonally and there was no way around. Violet chose instead to dismount and walk her bike down.

She was watching her tires, making sure they didn't catch in a gully, when something pulled her attention upward. A gray-brown squirrel was leaping through the branches overhead, as if afraid to touch the ground.

Violet opened her mouth to tell Caleb about it, when she saw a gully snag his front tire. His bike slammed to a stop, but Caleb didn't turn loose of his handlebars. He somersaulted forward and pulled the bike down atop him. Luckily, the path wasn't too steep. He didn't slide far.

Violet dropped her own bike and rushed forward to lift the bike off Caleb. Then she stood back, not sure how to touch him that wouldn't hurt. "Are you all right?"

He sprawled on his back, but none of his limbs seemed unnaturally bent. His eyes found hers. She saw a moment of pain in them, then he exaggerated his grimace.

"What a way to impress a girl," he groaned. He lifted one hand to her. She took it and pulled gently, more to balance him than to actually lift him to his feet.

"Thanks." He bent gingerly to brush the dirt from his jeans.

"Let's go back," Violet said. "Maybe you should see a doctor."

"I'm okay." Caleb stooped over his bike. The inner tube of the front tire had clearly popped.

They walked their bikes farther down the hill. Redwood trees towered above the path and closed out the sun.

Something streaked across the trail, left to right, a golden creature low to the ground. "Did you see that?" Violet asked, but Caleb was studying his wounded bike.

"What was it?" He looked up at her, then followed the direction of her gaze.

"Like a dog, I think." But its face wasn't doglike, was it? She frowned. "It was golden." She meant it burned like gold, like a figure made of sunlight.

"Maybe it was a coyote," Caleb said. "That's cool."

When they reached the place where she'd seen the animal, the hillside rose steeply to the left of the path and slanted away abruptly on the right. There was no way that an animal could have run along the trajectory she'd seen it on.

"I think the acid's kicking in," Violet observed.

"So soon?" Caleb wondered.

Just ahead of them, the ground dropped away in a series of uneven stone steps. The forest opened to reveal a body of water below them. Its surface, flecked with fallen leaves, reflected a patch of blue sky.

"Did you know this was here?" Violet asked, awed.

"It used to be the old swimming pool," Caleb said. "For the mansion. Two people supposedly drowned in it."

"Really?"

"That's what I heard."

"A swim would feel good," Violet said. She felt sticky after the ride up the mountain.

"Help me get my bike down the steps first," Caleb said. "I want to see if I can fix it before the acid makes me not care."

It was awkward to carry the broken bike down the uneven steps. Violet didn't see how he was going to repair its bent wheel, even if he could patch the inner tube. Probably it would be smart for them to turn around and head down the mountain now, since they were going to have to walk, but she really didn't want to leave. The acid made her feel jittery, quivering like a leaf on a breeze, and she didn't want to deal with cars or people or asphalt or the hairpin turns of the road now. She wanted to sit and look at the water.

A rough wall of fitted stones surrounded the path around the pool. Violet slung off her messenger bag and used the wall as a table. Then she bent to unlace her Chucks and strip off her socks.

The dirt path between the wall and the pool was warm beneath her sweaty feet. It hummed in the sunlight, alive and full of potential. Violet closed her eyes, but colors danced inside her mind, invading the peace she'd sought. It was more peaceful to open her eyes and gaze around.

Leaves drifted gently across the glassy surface of the water. Some of them splayed open like the fingers on severed hands. The image made her shiver, but when she stared at them, they returned to just being leaves.

Violet looked for steps down into the water itself but could see none. All the same, more gray stones fit together to form walls for the pool, going straight down until they vanished beneath the water. It really was a pool, she realized, rather than a pond. Manmade. The water looked so cool and inviting. There wasn't a lick of breeze down in this basin among the trees. The sun blazed down from high overhead, bright yellow, glaring in angry triangles from the water's surface. Violet wondered if she could tie her bandana over her eyes to protect them, but realized the blindfold wouldn't protect her from the colors inside her head.

"This stuff is really strong," she said or whispered or maybe only thought. Caleb didn't respond at all.

So she crouched at the edge of the pool. She wanted so much to put her feet in the water. Was it warm from the sun? Cool from a spring hidden below the surface? Would the water welcome her?

Two people drowned here, her thoughts reminded. Maybe they haunted the place. Maybe they'd grab her ankles, pull her in. Maybe the angry sun was actually warning her, trying to protect her...

She stuck one toe into the water, poised to yank it back if anything threatened. Nothing did. The water was lovely, just a little cool, like a blessing. Like a balm. Violet shivered with pleasure and added her other foot to the pool.

The sun slipped slowly behind a tree on the ridge above her. Once the glare had faded, Violet looked around in wonder. So beautiful here, each leaf crisp with IMAX 3D, shades of green she had no name for, browns so warm that she could wear them like skin. She felt such an immense wash of peace that she couldn't even remember if she had a problem somewhere else, somewhere distant. She wanted to live forever right here, right now, in this glorious moment. She offered the feeling up like a prayer, with gratitude.

She heard Caleb trying his cell phone, but he cursed it, unable to get any reception. Her attention was stolen by a big shiny black ant, who zigzagged across her leg like he was spelling out a warning.

A bubble popped on the water, but she didn't see what made it. When she looked back, the ant had gone.

Caleb sat cross-legged at her side. "The bike is fucked," he said. "I patched the tire, but the frame is bent."

"I'm sorry," she said, but that wasn't adequate. It was hard to force herself to care. "Give me a bit and I'll ride home and see if my brother can drive up here and get you."

"Not yet," Caleb said. "I'm really fucked up. I don't want him to see me like this."

Good, Violet thought. She didn't want to see anyone like this, either. She wasn't sure she could ride.

The sun peeked around a tree. Its warmth smothered her like a wool blanket. Sweat felt syrupy on her skin. Violet peeled her T-shirt over her head, intending to soak it in the pond and put it back on, but Caleb's hands undid the clasp of her bra.

She considered protesting. Did she want this? Not want this? But while she puzzled over it, his mouth sealed over her breast. Unexpected electricity jolted through her and disrupted her objections.

Everything seemed to happen in slow motion, or else her consciousness skipped from image to image like flipping through photographs. She and Caleb fumbled out of their clothing. They made a nest. He pillowed his head on her shoes.

Then she was atop him. He was inside her. It felt good, but she kept losing the thread. It wasn't building to anything. She closed her eyes against the bright blue sky. Images and colors poured into her mind. Symbols shifted and danced and seemed to coalesce. Like a spell, maybe, some kind of magic. A summoning? An invocation? She didn't feel a sense of calling, but there was an overwhelming feeling of generating something, creating something. Something powerful.

Caleb pulled away from her. It took Violet a moment to realize he'd finished. She shifted and he stood up, moved away, went to pee into the bushes.

Violet sat up herself, unfinished. She would have kept going all afternoon, but she knew poor Caleb couldn't keep up. It didn't really matter. Power tingled through her. She felt incandescent.

A trio of deer suddenly flashed by on the opposite side of the pool. They moved so quickly that Violet didn't get a clear glimpse of anything but their rolling eyes, white showing around the brown. They were terrified.

Her heart thrashed into a new rhythm. Terrified of what?

A mountain lion sprang off the boulder at the far end of the pool. It hung in the air a moment, claws extended, teeth flashing white. Violet didn't even have time to scream.

It knocked Caleb off his feet, rode him to the paving stones, its teeth buried in his neck. He squealed in a horrific high-pitched way that she knew she would never unhear.

Violet took stock in flashes: naked, no shoes, no weapons, no cell reception, no idea where she'd left her bike. Could she outride a mountain lion up the rutted path to the mansion? Would the abandoned house protect her or would the cat stalk her inside?

Caleb writhed more feebly now. The cat had him pinned face down. It worried its head back and forth, chewing through his spine.

Violet leapt to her feet.

Equally fast, the lion raised its head, yellow eyes slitted. Its tail whipped from side to side. *Run*, it dared her.

Violet flung herself the opposite direction, into the pool. She didn't think mountain lions swam. Only tigers swam, right? All other cats hated water.

The water was so cold that it nearly shocked her sober. It stole the breath from her in a big silver bubble that rose past her eyes, the only thing she could see in the murk.

The water was full of…things. Something brushed Violet's scissoring legs. It felt like hair. She would have screamed, if she'd had any air left.

Instead, she fought toward the surface. The tendrils let her go.

Her head broke through to the air and she coughed. It was

hard to coordinate her limbs. As she flailed, she remembered the people who might or might not have drowned in the pool. Would she join them in the shadows below?

Calm down, she ordered herself. *Dog paddle.*

She'd gotten turned around. All she saw was a hillside full of redwood trees. Peaceful. Green.

Maybe it hadn't really happened. Maybe she was tripping. Maybe she imagined the deer, the lion, the hideous keening. Maybe, any moment, Caleb would jump into the water beside her.

Slowly, she forced herself to rotate in the pool.

Two large kittens had crept from the forest now. One lapped at the blood flowing from Caleb's shredded neck. The other tore a chunk from his thigh.

The mama sat on Caleb's shoulders, watching Violet with golden eyes.

Something brushed her leg. Violet kept treading water, legs pedaling below her, but wondered: did the pool have leeches in it? Snapping turtles? Her thoughts darted into paranoia: were there sharks? Piranhas? Anything that might bite?

Not that it mattered. She would stay in this water and be gummed to death by goldfish rather than get out and take her chances with the mountain lion watching her from the side of the pool.

Whatever it was below her tangled in her toes. It felt for all the world like hair. Violet shuddered, losing her rhythm momentarily, but then forced her legs to scissor once more.

She peered down into the murky water. Something below her glowed an icy white color, like moonlight. Like the moon had fallen into the old swimming pool. The temperature of the water around her plummeted. A cramp knotted her left calf. Violet whimpered.

Her head dipped toward the surface of the water. Violet fought to calm herself, to hold herself up by the determined stroking of her arms. She tried to stretch the charley horse from her muscle.

Something very much like a hand touched her thigh.

She shrieked. The sound echoed from the hills surrounding

the pool and repeated from the mountain peak on the other side of the valley.

The mountain lion narrowed her eyes and stared at Violet.

Then a girl's voice said in her ear: "Don't be afraid."

Ice flooded her veins and Violet lost the ability to control her limbs. Her head slipped under the surface of the water and she took a breath…and something caught her in its arms and lifted her, coughing, back to the surface. And held her there, safely, until she could breathe again.

Violet's heart fluttered in her chest, struggling to regain its rhythm. She could see arms around her ribs, holding her up in the water. They were a pale grayish white. *Not a natural color.* She wondered if it was possible to die of fear.

"Don't be afraid of me," the ghost said gently. "I won't hurt you."

"I'm afraid to look at you," Violet whispered. She didn't trust her own voice, didn't want to hear the sound of her own terror.

"I'm not horrible," the ghost promised.

"Did you drown here?"

"A long time ago."

Violet swallowed hard. Her throat was sore from the water she'd inhaled. She coughed once more, but it didn't really help. Tentatively, she started to dog paddle.

The ghost released her. Violet turned slowly, to find a girl her own age bobbing alongside her. Her long, long hair was blond, where Violet's was dark. It was slicked to her skull and green with streaks of pondweed. Her eyes were pale blue, maybe, or green, where Violet's were brown. The drowned girl *wasn't* horrible, even if her skin had gone the color of something kept from sunlight for a long, long time.

"Are you alone here?" Violet asked. The quaver in her voice unnerved her even more, if that were possible. She swallowed again and tried to concentrate on her kicking.

"My boyfriend is here, too," the ghost said. "He doesn't like to talk to people."

"Did you die together?"

"We thought it would be romantic," the ghost said. "We

didn't realize we'd be trapped here. That's why I don't want you to die. You will be trapped here, too."

"Why are you trapped?"

"A creature roams these woods. A monster. It is hungry for company. It collects us."

"How many of you are there?" Violet asked, even though she didn't want to know the answer.

"Lots," the ghost said sadly. "Lots."

"I don't want to be trapped here," Violet said, "but I don't know how to get past the mountain lion."

"There is no mountain lion," the ghost said. "That's the monster. It takes many forms."

Violet remembered the thing she'd seen as she and Caleb walked their bikes down to the pool, the doglike creature that crossed their paths at the impossible angle. Her heart fluttered again. The monster had been tracking them for hours, ever since they walked past the abandoned house. Why hadn't it attacked while Caleb was fixing his bike? Why hadn't it attacked while they were making love?

Because, Violet thought, both those times she had been praying. At first, she had been overwhelmed by the beauty of the summer's day, the sunlight shimmering through the leaves of the trees. Then she had been blissed out on the sensations in her body, the colors exploding in her head. She had been adrift in joy at those moments, full of life.

And that had protected her.

Somewhere, deep in her mind, a dark little voice cautioned: *Do you hear how crazy that sounds? That's some kind of stupid hippie bullshit. It's going to get you killed.*

Violet squashed those thoughts, silenced the voice. She couldn't wait for the mountain lion to finish eating her boyfriend and drag his body off into the woods. She'd get tired of swimming and would drown long before then. She could not rely on the kindness of ghosts to save her. She had to get out of this pool, put on her clothing, grab her bike, and ride out of here. She had to do it before dark, because she could not spend the night treading water in a haunted pool. She had to do it alone, because no one knew where she was. No one was going to come rescue her.

The shadows of the trees had grown visibly longer, as the sun sank toward the mountain's peak. Soon there would be no more sunlight on the water.

Something bright skimmed across the surface of the pool toward her. When it got close enough, it resolved into a pale blue dragonfly. Its wings made a rattle like cellophane. They flickered with rainbows, prisming in the last of the afternoon light.

"Hello," Violet said gently. And she felt the wonder and joy begin to fill her again. She lifted her hand out of the water, held it up, and the dragonfly perched there, lighter than a scrap of paper. It looked at her steadily and that, for some mad reason, gave her courage.

She wished she had some way to distract the monster. If there had been a stick floating on the surface of the pond, she would have tried throwing it into the bushes. That probably wouldn't work, but she would've tried anything. If she still had her shoes on, she would have sacrificed one...

She scanned the area around the pond. Her clothing sprawled at the rim of the pool: tennis shoes, jeans, panties, T-shirt. Her messenger bag was there, too.

Up the rough stone steps, then. She could just see the front tire of her bike, parked on the path. She would need to scoop up her clothing, sprint up the steps, turn the bike around, and ride off up the hill faster than the creature could leap after her.

A second dragonfly buzzed over. The first lifted off from her fingers. Together, they circled her head, like a crown. Like an aura. Like a halo. Violet smiled.

"Yes," the ghost said. "You can do it."

Violet felt the drug spinning inside her body. It wasn't carried in her bloodstream any longer. It had become part of her every cell, dancing in orbit around every nucleus. She stroked strongly through the water toward the edge of the pool and her clothing.

The mountain lion watched her curiously, but didn't move.

Violet took a deep breath, feeding her body with oxygen, transmuting it inside her skin to fire. Then she thrust herself up out of the water and clambered over the rough stone edge of the pool.

She bent to collect her clothing.

The mountain lion stretched lazily, front claws flexed to scrape on the stone.

Violet snatched up her messenger bag and shoved her clothes inside. Her knuckles struck her Swiss Army knife. She pulled it out.

The mountain lion paced toward her.

Violet turned toward it, met its eyes, and smiled. She opened the knife and let the sunlight flash on its blade. She felt mean. Fierce. Ready to beat the living crap out of the monster if only it came within reach. Maybe she'd rethink the vegetarian thing, too.

The lion faltered, confused.

"Come at me," Violet dared. "I will rip you to fucking pieces. I will sit on your back and bite through your spine."

One of the babies sprang toward her playfully. Violet looked down at it, then up at the mother.

"Call it back," Violet threatened. "Or it's going into the pool and my friends down there will have a kitten to play with."

The creature watched her, measuring, then made a low grumble that clearly expressed her displeasure. The cub turned immediately and scampered back to hide between its mother's paws.

"So you do understand me," Violet said. "Then understand this: I'm leaving. You're going to let me go. You are not going to follow me. You are not going to stop me or get in my way or pounce on me once my back is turned. I am going to be safe from you and your children, or so help me, I will be the last person you ever fuck with."

The mountain lion bent down to gently lift the cub in her mouth. She turned and calmly walked away, each powerful muscle gliding smoothly as water beneath her skin. The other kitten loped after them.

Violet scrambled into her T-shirt and jeans, but didn't worry about her shoes or underwear. Then she sprinted up the steps and jumped on her bike and pedaled out of there, up the hill, as fast as the proverbial bat.

She hadn't gone too far when she realized she'd better slow

down or she was going to wreck her bike like Caleb did.

Which led her to think about Caleb. What had really happened to him? Had he really been killed? Had he really been eaten?

The breath hitched in her chest, but she shoved the emotion down. First she had to get away. Then she had to tell someone what had happened. Then they would come back and get Caleb's body and see if they could find his ghost and if they could free it from that monster…if they could free all the ghosts and send them to their rest.

No one is ever going to believe you, hissed a nasty voice in her head. *They'll think you killed him.*

Except for the fang marks, she told it.

They'll think you're a coward for leaving him behind.

Anyone would run from a mountain lion, unless they had a better weapon than a pocketknife.

They'll think you're a slut. A drug addict. A junkie whore.

Violet reached the old house and made the turn back onto the driveway that would lead her to the road. Houses. People. Safety.

She refused to be ashamed for liking Caleb, for having sex with him. He'd been a good friend, someone she could be quiet with. Someone who didn't mock her love of nature, or drugs, or sex.

Tears prickled her eyes. She slowed her pace even more. If she lost it now, it was a long, dangerous ride back down the mountain. Road rash would slow her down as much as a broken bike.

Didn't the boy she'd loved deserve to be grieved? Didn't she owe him that?

Yes. Later, when she was safe.

It wasn't like she'd lured him to his death. He brought her up here. He knew how wild it was. Maybe he knew how haunted it was, too. It wasn't like she'd had any idea of the risks before she'd said yes to a bike ride and some acid in the woods on a sunny day.

Now that she knew the risks, she wondered if she would ever have the courage to ride on the mountain or through the woods again.

She reached the road and turned downward. It swooped gently around a stand of redwoods. Beyond them, the view lay revealed: the town below stretched away toward the bay. San Francisco shimmered in the distance. Maybe she'd move to the city, she told herself. Across the water, where it was safe.

She turned one last time for a glimpse of the abandoned house. In its highest window, under the eaves, stood a woman. One child snuggled in her arms. Another leaned against her thigh. Three pairs of unblinking golden eyes watched Violet.

Violet knew she would have to come back. She would have to rescue Caleb's ghost and she owed the girl in the pool, too. She had a lot to learn before that. The monster wouldn't let her go a second time without a fight.

The woman in the window smiled. *Come back any time*, she said. Violet heard her very clearly. Shivering, she pedaled off down the mountain.

In the Pines

Haylie felt herself vanishing into her math homework. The numbers were as concrete as the desk in front of her, brought to life by the soft warm glow of the desk lamp gilding her math book. Haylie was desperate to sink into the problems, solve them, move on. So different than real life.

Eventually she even tuned out the music playing on her phone, something her friend Kat had suggested to help her keep calm. It took Haylie a while to surface from working the final problem. Gradually, she became aware of something scratching against her windowpane.

The snowstorm was bad tonight: four inches of snow predicted, maybe more. Haylie hoped the weather woman was wrong. She hoped the worst of the storm would pass them by. The last thing she wanted was a snow day, forced to stay home with her weeping mother and shouting father. She'd much rather be at school, where work might at least take her mind off of things.

The storm scratched more insistently at her window, dragging her away from the final math problem again. Sighing, Haylie tugged an earbud from one ear.

Her room faced Magnolia Street. The old oak tree in the front yard remembered the Civil War. Maybe the wind was enough to make its twigs scratch at her window.

When she twisted in her desk chair, the shadow outside the window startled her. Amidst the swirling flakes of snow, the shadow raised a hand again to tap on the window glass.

Haylie almost called her dad. As the sound rose in her throat, she realized she didn't want him here in her cozy room, stomping and shouting and watching her as if she was going to disappear.

The shadow put its face closer to the glass. The desk lamp's glow reflected from ice crystals in Miria's hair, like diamonds in her black curls.

Haylie jumped up to open the window to let her sister in. In her haste, the earbud's cord snagged on the desk lamp. The lamp toppled over to crash against her math homework. Shaken loose in its socket, the bulb went dark.

Again Haylie almost shouted. Again she stopped herself. She didn't want to set her mother off on another crying jag.

She reached out to turn the window's lock, but the jamb had swollen in the cold. Although she yanked on it, the window wouldn't open.

"You're going to have to push," she said, sure that her voice was too soft for Miria to hear over the storm. Haylie didn't want their dad to overhear. Until she made sure her sister was okay, she didn't want her parents to intrude. She was desperate for a moment with Miria all to herself, before the world crashed in. She wanted a world without TV cameras and police lights.

Miria put her hands flat against the wooden frame and shoved as Haylie heaved. The window popped open abruptly. Haylie stumbled backward, collided with the bed, and sat down hard.

Although Miria waited outside, the snow didn't. It flew into the room, melting as it fell against Haylie's face.

"What are you waiting for?" Haylie gasped, struggling off of the bed. "A personal invitation?" That was something her dad said. She grimaced. "Come in and close the window before we get in trouble."

Miria slithered in. She moved in a weird boneless way, stretching one leg down until her toes touched the carpeted floor, then sliding the other leg in and down before drawing her torso after her.

Instead of the purple Converse high-tops that Miria always wore, she had on a pair of black leather boots with sharply pointed toes and even sharper heels. Haylie asked, "Where did you get those boots, Miria?"

"In the pines." Her sister's throaty voice was almost unfamiliar.

Haylie finally untangled her feet from the comforter. She reached over to turn on the floor lamp standing beside the bed.

Her sister wore a tiny shimmery dress, barely longer than a bath towel. What Haylie had taken for snow crystals on the fabric were actually little glass beads, black on black. The dress made her sister look older than fourteen. Haylie would have sworn Miria was wearing makeup too, bruise-purple shadow and a lipstick that gave her mouth a bluish tinge.

"Where did you get that dress?" Haylie asked.

"In the pines."

Was that a store? Haylie didn't know it, but she'd never been very interested in shopping and girlie things. She hadn't thought Miria was, either.

"Where have you been?" Haylie demanded. "Mom and Dad have been sick with worry. The cops have been here I don't know how many times. We drove all over town, putting up posters and handing out flyers. They've even been on the news."

Miria stared at her, but didn't answer.

The icy wind whistled through the room. Miria made no attempt to shut the window behind her. Haylie wanted to reach past her sister to close the window, but something held her back, kept her standing in the circle of light thrown by the floor lamp.

"Where did you sleep last night?" Haylie whispered.

"In the pines," Miria said. "In the pines, where the sun never shines."

"Dressed like that?" Haylie asked.

"I shivered when the cold wind blew."

Haylie stared at her sister. In the back of her mind, she could almost hear a song that echoed the things Miria said. Maybe the bruises around Miria's eyes weren't makeup. Maybe Miria's lips had gone blue.

Her parents were just downstairs, watching TV and waiting for news about Miria. Haylie knew she could call them. Dad would clomp up the stairs and shout at Miria and Mom would hang in the doorway and start crying again...

Whatever happened next, Haylie knew it would be awful.

The doorbell rang downstairs. Before anyone could move to answer it, someone pounded on the door. It was the police. That's what the police did whenever they thought they had a lead about her sister.

"My baby!" their mother wailed downstairs. Their father yelled for Haylie to come down.

"You coming?" Haylie asked.

Miria shook her head and held out her hand. There was dirt under her broken fingernails.

The cold wind howled through Haylie's room. Both of them shivered.

The Acid That Dissolves Images

You throw the magazine into the jumble of makeup heaped beneath the mirror. "Pretentious gory poseur," the critic called you, "bastard love-child of Alice Cooper, Marilyn Manson, and the whole 20th-century shock-rock scene." You draw a (hopefully) calming breath. The critic obviously hadn't stayed for the whole show.

Obviously. Medusa is an angry itch inside you, mixed in the bile that creeps up the back of your throat. You suck miserably on a beer, but the bitter taste won't go away. How long can this sane front hold?

Your hands shake as you load the gun. The first bullet shatters the mirror, your reflection; the second silences the digiplayer. As Medusa rises, you feel the hardness returning. It feels *good*.

Medusa wonders: if she shot the body you share in the shoulder, could you still go on stage—despite the pain, despite your arm hanging incarnadine against the shiny black latex catsuit? You wish there were some way to shoot her. Instead, you hold the magazine at arm's length and blow it to confetti. It snows down around you, smelling of cordite.

Over the dressing room intercom, Carl asks, "Are you ready, Rachel?"

In response, Medusa laughs. Her low, cruel cackle has become your trademark.

To invite him in, you promise, "I won't shoot you." Still, the creature inside you might, just to see how Carl would meet death. He is one of the few young men you know, a conscientious objector. A couple of months ago, he claimed he would rather report to prison—with all that entailed—than join the Army. But the night his draft notice came, Medusa plucked out his eyes on stage. Carl fainted before she finished the first one.

He can't afford cybernetic replacements, of course, and the Army won't lay out that kind of cash for a grunt they don't expect to see again once they dump him in the desert.

You've been wondering why Carl stayed in the band. Maybe, in a twisted way, he is grateful to Medusa. He's as friendly to you as anyone dares to be these days.

Carl opens the dressing room door. He seems to regard you through the gauze that covers his empty sockets. "Did you read the review in *Modern Image*?" he asks.

You decide to be honest. "Why did our first national publicity have to be a slam?"

"Any mention is better than no mention at all." Carl crosses his arms on his chest and leans against the doorframe. "Sounded to me like she made up her mind about us before the show started, then left after the first song. They call the magazine *Image*, not *Substance*." He smiles. "It hasn't affected the size of tonight's crowd. Maybe it helped."

You wish he hadn't told you that. Medusa has gotten really wild on the nights she's had a big audience. Last time it was Carl. How can she top that? Feigning calm, you jab the pointed nail of your little finger at your eyelashes, forcing the mascara to spike still more. Finally you say *screwit* and pull the bone-white shock of bangs into your face. These normal gestures do not faze Medusa. She shows you white hair clotted with crimson. Behind it, your shattered reflection wears Medusa's smile.

You follow Carl backstage. The cinderblocks of the hall are covered with the graffiti of a hundred bands. Most of the names are unfamiliar. When you reach the wings, the effluvia of spilled beer and hair mousse washes over you. You envision the crowd: witch bitches in their black gowns and silver talismans, knots of mohawked punks, a tourist or two in bondage gear. Desperate women, wanting a spectacle to make them forget how lonely they are, how long ago their men disappeared into the desert. Carl gets laid every night. So does the computer jockey, Ann. It seems forever since you've had anybody but Medusa for company.

The band stands in a clump, passing a joint of Lydia's one-hit weed. Though excluded, you bask in their camaraderie. Again you are glad to have answered their ad for a singer. The performances allow you respite from Medusa, when you don't need to clutch her leash so tightly. Still, now that she's grown abusive of this freedom, perhaps you *should* quit.

"Poseur," Medusa murmurs. *"You would quit after one scathing review. I don't need you holding me back any longer."*

You realize Medusa still holds the gun. You thrust it through the back of your belt and hope she will forget about it. How likely is that? Still, she can't kill you. She needs you to move around in. And she needs the band, to do whatever it is she's come to do. You promise yourself that they'll be safe.

The houselights dim. The audience rustles, a thousand-eyed beast whose attention is suddenly focused. Your fingertips are icy as you slip the microphone over your head, switch on the box of effects at your hip. "I'll show you gore," Medusa teases. You wish you knew what she is planning, but you never do.

The machines kick on, spewing pale smoke that smells like myrrh. In the gloom, Ann's computer lights glow a malevolent red. Lydia leads Carl to his drums, waits solicitously for him to find the controls. Then she lifts her bass from its cradle and turns up the volume.

A moan begins, like a graveyard wind. Lydia weaves in a rapid bass melody.

When the fog reaches your knees, you pace slowly to downstage middle. Thus ends the rehearsed part of the show.

"Is ecstasy possible in destruction?" Medusa whispers through the effects box. The reverse reverb repeats each word, clarifying it before biting it off. "Can one grow young in cruelty?"

Fear becomes a chill rock in your stomach.

"Do you desire to see the Truth?" Medusa asks.

A stark white spotlight pierces the smoke to strike harsh reflections off the shiny latex catsuit. With one hand, Medusa forces your head back, caresses your throat, cups one breast, hugs your bony ribs. Yes, she is killing you. You shiver, not altogether in fear.

"Do you desire essential satisfaction?" Medusa purrs. "I do."

With a savage tug, she rips an earring from your left ear, throws it to the stage, and mashes the silver nude beneath her boot. Blood drips on your neck, warm and sensual. Medusa touches her fingers to it, brushes it across your lips. Delicious.

"Let us enjoy ourselves to the full. 'Tis Nature's law."

Medusa steals lyrics from Rimbaud, Crowley, Huysmans, everyone you've read. She has an incredible memory for cruelty.

Women crowd around the stage. Someone thrusts a black-gloved fist into the spotlight. You wonder what they derive from Medusa, why her fury attracts and binds them, mothlike, as it does you. Medusa only smiles.

A flashbulb dazzles your eyes.

Medusa stalks toward the flash, hissing lines from *The Torture Garden* into the microphone. The crowd washes after her, waves against the breakwater of the stage.

She halts, swaying on stiletto boot heels. Anger pounds like a bass drum inside your skull. You have to fight her to see.

The fortyish woman holds a camera at arm's length over her head and snaps another picture. Trendy gold fans shield her ears. Her painstakingly ratted hair glows plum in the lights. You recognize her as the critic from *Modern Image. Why could she be here*, Medusa demands, *unless to see if she has destroyed you?*

Now that she has your attention, the critic shouts something. Sandwiched chest-high against the stage by the crowd, she is white-faced. You can't hear her over the Berlioz melody Ann's computer is generating. As you bend close to the footlights, Medusa switches on the flanger.

"They're crushing me. I can't catch my breath," the critic gasps. Your microphone Doppler-shifts the words, giving them a ghostly echo.

Like a bird of prey, Medusa's laugh spirals up over the effects. She strides across the stage to Carl, drapes her arms over his shoulders, pinches his nipples through his black T-shirt. He freezes, rigid against your chest. "Count yourself lucky, bitch," Medusa snarls. "Some people can't see."

Abandoning Carl, Medusa adjusts the effects control slightly. When she speaks, a Medusan chorus speaks with her. "I don't recommend leaving tonight's show early. That pisses me off."

You pray that Medusa is smart enough to leave the critic alone.

Someone shimmies over the edge of the stage. The girl has the angular hips of a voluptuous figure starved to thinness. Her clinging black velour jumpsuit is a cheap imitation of your latex. Like yours, her bangs are bleached bone-white. With a jolt, you recall the vision in the dressing room: the bloody white bangs.

Ann kicks in some heavy trumpets, guiding Carl into a dance beat.

You near the girl to find her quoting de Sade's *Juliette*. Medusa embraces her so that she can be heard over the microphone.

The girl falters, more interested in kissing the blood from your neck. Medusa trumps the quotation with more de Sade. "To judge whether love be madness, is not the lover's distraction sufficient proof of it?"

She yanks the girl's head back by the hair, then kisses her. The sound, multiplied by the chorus, becomes horrible, obscene. Ann has recorded the quote and feeds it through her sampler, breaking the words apart and reordering them.

You turn your back on the girl and dance to Ann's infectious music. Lydia grins with relief.

The girl rips the handgun from your belt, rattling the delicate effects box in the process. You spin. She is taking exaggerated aim across the footlights at the critic. Lydia's fingers stumble on the bass strings, but Carl's drumbeat is steady. "Sufficient proof?" asks the computer.

Medusa walks into the firing line.

Had she been serious in the dressing room about shooting you, about seeing your blood against the latex? Inside her, you are shrieking: *Don't be stupid! Killing me won't convince the critic you're not a poseur.*

"I'm not a poseur," Medusa says. *"You,* of all people, should know that."

The girl gazes at you with confused eyes the heart-stabbing blue of a mountain lake. Medusa quotes Crowley again: "Do what thou wilt shall be the whole of the Law." Through the shaken effects box, her voice sounds masculine, infinitely jaded, alien.

Panicking, you try to throw yourself out of harm's way. But

Medusa is stronger, has always been stronger. Your body only sways. Death stares at you with the circular bore of the gun.

"Do what thou wilt," Medusa repeats.

The girl smiles as if Medusa has blessed her, given her something she never hoped to have. You struggle to speak the words to take back the gift, words that could save her, that would save yourself. You hear Medusa's cackle.

For an instant, you see Medusa through the girl's adoring eyes. You find Medusa as beautiful as fresh blood against white porcelain, as a drop shimmering at the tip of a hypodermic, as a star-filled breeze through a penthouse window. She is final. You are obsolete. Awestruck, overwhelmed, indebted, you embrace Medusa for the first time.

The change is instantaneous and merciful, like the bullet the girl puts into her own heart.

Medusa lifts the dead girl in her arms, smearing blood against the latex catsuit. In her own voice, without effects, Medusa paraphrases Artaud, speaking in funereal time over Carl's drumbeat. "It is I who have committed suicide today, torn myself from my body, battled against myself, wishing never to come back to myself."

A flashbulb goes off, then dozens of them, like heat lightning.

Elemental, primal, unleashed, Medusa regards her worshippers and considers what she will do next.

Valentine

Alondra had never done this kind of magic before. It felt awful, dirty. Her head ached from the concentration it took. Still, she sat in the quaint café, drinking peppermint tea. Teeth gritted, she traced sigils for summoning in the moisture her glass left on the birch tabletop.

She'd never been to Oslo before, spoke almost no Norwegian, but that hadn't posed a problem. The Scandinavians she'd met all spoke lovely English. It shamed her to not have more vocabulary. She'd scarcely prepared for the trip and didn't know how long before her quarry moved on.

And he traveled a lot. Alondra wasn't sure if he fled something or searched for something. Not that it mattered. She didn't want to know more about him than his regular habits in this place. She needed to know enough to find him. Meet him. Get him alone and kill him.

Cold sweat slicked her hands on the glass of tea. Murder was so out of character that she could barely hold the thought long enough to plan. Still, she had no other option. Victor needed a new heart and she would bring him one. It was the least she could do.

But...murder?

How would she live with the deed? She wouldn't be able to tell Victor what she'd done. She probably wouldn't even be able to face him. She vowed to do this thing, get it over with, save Victor's life, and run. She'd find somewhere deep and dark in which to hide. Then she would never, ever return home. It would be enough to know that Victor survived.

She drained the glass of tea and signaled for another, then resumed drawing sigils on the tabletop.

She stared into space, focus lost, when something called her back to the low-ceilinged room. Nearby, hunched over a tall pint of Ringnes, sat Simon Lebranche. Her target.

Hers weren't the only eyes drawn to him. He didn't make a spectacle of himself, but he also didn't blend in. He'd shed his big fur coat: beaver? otter? Something lush and dark, anyway. Beside his beer glass sat a black silk cavalier's hat, complete with ostrich plume. He wore a black sweater soft as cashmere, over black leather jeans heavy enough to block the cold. All the black clothing set off his creamy skin, his chartreuse eyes, his tousled hair and beard like spun gold.

Alondra didn't know how old Lebranche was. She'd read that he'd fired his musket at the Battle of Marsten Moor, fought on horseback at Jasna Góra and later at Waterloo. Never on the winning side, but always surviving to fight again. After Napoleon's defeat, Lebranche had taken an interest in the arts, befriending Dante Gabriel Rossetti, even posing for him. Now all that seemed gone: friends, war, art. Maybe he searched for someone to end his wandering.

Alondra didn't have to resort to her second sight to see the energy coursing around him—Saint Elmo's fire—sparking and spitting in the dark café. The wonder was that no one else saw it. That kind of life force was perfect for her needs, as long as she didn't panic and fuck it up.

Lebranche caught her looking and swiveled the chair next to him invitingly.

Alondra swept her hand across the liquid on the tabletop and collected her things. She slipped into the vacant chair while Lebranche gazed out the window at the Museum of Contemporary Art's sculpture garden across the street.

"Do you know me?" His accent was vaguely French and half a hundred other things.

"I'd like to," she purred, then wondered if she'd overdone it. She watched the path his hand took to lift his beer.

"You can see it, then?"

He didn't mean his hand. Alondra nodded. "I see it. Like a corona around the sun."

"Like a moth to a flame?" he asked. He seemed too weary to threaten her.

"Like used to surround my boyfriend, only his energy was red. He was a vampire."

"Was?" Lebranche echoed.

"May still be." She shrugged. "He left me when I refused to become a vampire, too."

Alondra had considered tracking Jordan down, even though she didn't bear a grudge. An immortal she knew would have been easier to trap, if not to kill. She'd decided that she didn't want to infect Victor with vampirism. She didn't know if such a thing could be transmitted via organ transplant, but didn't assume there'd been much research on the topic.

"Why didn't you join him?" Lebranche asked. "Doesn't everyone crave immortality?"

He amused himself at her expense, but rather than let on that she understood his subtext, Alondra took the question at face value. "I couldn't stand the intimacy drinking blood requires. You're not a vampire, are you?"

Lebranche laughed. "I didn't know there was such a thing."

He was lying. He must have seen them during his centuries at war, feeding on the fallen.

He noticed that she hadn't brought her tea. "Can I buy you a drink, Miss...?"

"DeCourval." She watched for a reaction, but he didn't acknowledge the name. "I've been here all afternoon. Would you like to go out?"

"I have drinking to do."

"How disappointing. It would be nice to feel today's moment of sunlight on my face."

"Get your coat, then."

Her hands sank deep into the coat as she lifted it from the chair. She loved the wolf's winter fur, its dense whiteness starred with longer hairs of silver and ash. The coat's icy color made her face rosy; pink as Empress Josephine's pearls, Victor used to say. It had been his gift, the year they'd gone to Moscow.

Lebranche helped her into the heavy fur. "Not many women wear wolf anymore. You didn't have a boyfriend who was a werewolf?"

"Not yet." She lifted her flame-red hair up over the coat's

collar, trailed it across his hands. "It was a gift."

"From your vampire?"

"Another older man."

"You like them older?"

Alondra laughed. "When you're my age, the only men of interest are older."

She twisted her hair into a coil and tucked it inside her coat. It made her anxious to wear her hair loose in public.

She wasn't sure if Lebranche meant merely to send her away, so she lingered over the coat's toggles, fastening herself up to brave the Norwegian winter. Still standing, Lebranche drained his pilsner. He put on his cavalier's hat. "You have a destination in mind?"

"I've wanted to see Vigeland Park."

"There's no drinking involved in that." He shouldered into his big black coat anyway.

"Bring a bottle along. They swear aquavit keeps people warm."

Vigeland Park was deserted in the watery sunlight. Snow balanced in precarious piles atop the statues. Gustav Vigeland spent the last half of his life making more than two hundred sculptures in granite and bronze, exploring relationships between men and women, life and death. The funny thing was that Alondra *had* actually wanted to see the park, although not so much under these circumstances. She'd heard it was beautiful.

"What's brought you to Oslo in the coldest part of the year?" Lebranche asked.

"My guardian is dying. I can't stand to watch."

Lebranche inclined his head but offered no false comfort. "Why Oslo?"

"He and I traveled a lot. We hadn't visited Oslo. I've got no history here." Alondra had practiced the lie, but even referencing Victor distressed her. She turned the question around. "Why are you here?"

Lebranche shrugged.

They strolled to the next cluster of snow-shrouded sculptures. Though the monolithic nudes retained the volume of the granite blocks from which they'd been hewn, the couples cradled each other tenderly. Alondra said, "You could have gone farther north."

"I would have missed you."

The way he said it charmed her. She didn't want to like Lebranche, to feel pity or compassion for him. She had a job to do.

He asked, "Did I say too much?"

Alondra forced a laugh. "I was wondering how to invite you back to my hotel. I was going to go with, 'Would you like to go somewhere warm?'"

"That would have worked," Lebranche encouraged. "Or you could have said: 'Simon, come back to my hotel.'"

Alondra leaned up to kiss him. His blond beard was softer than she expected, although icy from his breath. She wondered if he felt the cold.

His kiss was enthusiastic. Breathless, flustered, Alondra said, "Please come back to my hotel room, Simon."

"At your service."

She flung her wolf fur over the bed as Simon poked up the fire banked on the grate. Fireplaces in hotel rooms, what could be more welcome than that? Alondra took the shallow silver bowl from the rose-painted bureau. She filled it half-full of aquavit and knelt beside the fire.

From inside her emerald sweater, she pulled a gold chain. She twisted its pendant open to reveal a penknife. She slashed the blade across her right thumb, counted six fat red droplets into the bowl, then put the wound to her lips.

"What's that?"

Alondra met Simon's avid eyes over the thumb she was sucking. "Protection."

She lifted the bowl and drank deeply. The aquavit tasted like rye bread and burned like absinthe going down. She couldn't taste blood at all. The alcohol flushed her cheeks when she held the bowl out. "Leave some."

Simon gulped the spell down and handed the bowl back. A half-cup of liquor remained, enough for the task at hand. Alondra set the bowl on the fieldstone hearth and struck a match. Green flames danced across the surface of the alcohol.

"Now we won't be disturbed."

"Were you expecting to be disturbed?"

"I don't want any bad news tonight."

Now that the time had come to seduce him, Alondra found herself unnerved. She'd only had sex with three other men. One had not been consensual. Only one of the others had been especially gentle. She wasn't sure she wanted Simon to be gentle. In a way, she wanted him to be cruel, to punish her for what she meant to do.

"You don't often invite men to your hotel, do you?"

"Is it that obvious?"

"What do you hope will happen?"

"You'll warm me up."

"I can do that." He settled her in his lap, her back against his chest. Then he lifted her hair to kiss her neck. She shivered, amazed that he found something she liked on the first try. "Close your eyes," he directed. "Imagine I am whomever you want me to be."

"I was raped," she admitted, surprising herself with the honesty. "Sometimes, when I close my eyes, I see him."

Simon held her loosely, not confining her. He confessed, "I've been a rapist. Spoils of war."

"You've no doubt been many things."

He didn't answer. She realized she'd said too much, let him know she guessed more about him than a casual acquaintance would. Rather than compound the error, Alondra reached up to unhook her necklaces. She set them on the hearth, one by one. She wondered if he'd understand she was disarming herself. Removing her charms made her feel more naked than shedding her clothing would.

"You don't have to take those off if they make you feel safe," Simon said. She was surprised he grasped her sacrifice.

"Undress me," she whispered.

He reached under her sweater to unhook her bra. His hands were calloused, workman's hands. Her heart thudded. Alondra set aside the final necklace, then twisted to face him. Simon caressed her, stroking and teasing, trying to find a way to unlock her. Alondra studied his eyes, yellow-green as the sea before a storm. Crow's-feet folded around them when he smiled.

"Enough foreplay?"

"Yes."

"On the bed?"

Alondra shook her head as if at her own appetite. "I was imagining lying on your wonderful coat. It's too much to ask."

"Drag it down here in front of the fire."

Simon helped her spread the coat on the floor. Alondra lay on it, luxuriating in the deep fur against her bare back. Simon stood. He turned away modestly to strip off his leather jeans. Alondra admired his lovely backside. She shimmied out of her jeans while he wasn't watching.

When he turned back, he'd rolled on a condom. Alondra was sheltered enough that she hadn't seen one before, but guessed what she was looking at. The gesture touched her.

"I don't understand your reasons for this," Simon said softly, "but I'm grateful."

Alondra felt like a sacrifice, stretched across an altar. She was eager to begin, to have it over. While Simon wasn't unaware of that, he worked to ensure she took pleasure, too.

She clung to him, staring into the fire. She wanted him to enjoy himself, but this was all too sad and terrible. Eventually moved to the edge of orgasm when physical sensations outstripped her emotions, Alondra let a tear slip free. Simon paused, but Alondra let her body encourage him. After that, he put his cheek beside hers and held her tighter. She felt safe, protected, even loved. She hated him for making this so hard.

When they'd finished, her body felt deliciously languid, grateful for the momentary respite. She'd driven herself for months, obsessed with keeping Victor alive. All that seemed far away now. Alondra felt almost as good as when she'd drunk the elixir of life in Prague.

She wondered if that was Simon's secret: a philosopher's stone tucked in his clothing. Not that another stone would succeed where her own had failed. She hoped something else guaranteed Simon's long life. Something transferable.

He lay on his stomach on the coat, facing her. "Warm now?"

"Thank you."

He kissed her again. His body was long and muscular where hers was soft and rounded. Her flesh yearned for his warmth, for the comfort of his arms. She closed her eyes so that he wouldn't see her warring with herself. He'd treated her kindly. She felt wonderful. This was so wrong.

Then the bowl of aquavit flared, shooting up a six-inch spout of green flame before burning out.

Simon relaxed as if his strings had been cut. His green eyes stared sightlessly at her.

It crossed her mind that she didn't have to be alone; neither did Simon. This evening could heal them both. Maybe they could steal happiness from the universe, some mutual protection from the cold and dark. She was desperately tempted to let him live.

But Simon was a wanderer. He didn't—maybe couldn't—settle down. Alondra didn't want that for herself. She envisioned a little cottage somewhere, a garden, children, a handful of cats… In all his years, Simon had never chosen a home. Alondra didn't suppose she was the one to change what all others could not. Sure, she had magic on her side, but she didn't want to waste her life keeping a man.

Alondra crawled out from under Simon's arm. She struggled, but finally sprawled him onto his back. She hadn't taken into account how much bigger he was, close to six feet. All that muscle made him heavy.

His open eyes unsettled her. Alondra considered draping something over his face. Her sweater was close at hand. Simon was unconscious; how could he mind? In the end, she couldn't depersonalize him like that. This was a specific person: unique, as far as she knew. She owed him the dignity of dying like a man.

She went to her suitcase and retrieved Jordan's scalpel kit, the one he'd used for drinking blood. She brought it back and crouched over Simon's body. She didn't have anything to crack his sternum, so she'd have to come in from under the ribcage. She traced where his organs should be: stomach, liver, major pectoral artery. She didn't want to nick that. This would be messy enough without blood spraying around.

She reached for Simon's bottle of aquavit and had a healthy belt, for courage. Then she braided her hair, leaned forward, and made the first cut. The scalpel was sharp enough to penetrate with scarcely any force behind it. Blood spilled down Simon's ribs to pool in the black fur coat.

She made a cut big enough for her hand. She was pleased by how straight she'd made the incision. After this, maybe she'd go to medical school in São Paulo or Phuket. Maybe she'd become a surgeon like Victor's eldest son Michael. And fuck him anyway, while she thought of it. Stupid motherfucker wouldn't put his own father on the transplant list, no matter how Alondra begged.

While she wondered how to reach inside Simon's body and not slash the heart by accident, spoiling it, the edges of the cut shivered together, lining up cell by cell, healing before her eyes.

It fucking figured.

Would his heart heal as quickly, if she gashed it tearing it out?

Maybe he'd grow another heart to replace the one she was stealing. That was undoubtedly too much for which to hope.

She made another incision, right above the first. Before she lost her nerve, she thrust her hand into Simon's chest. Inside his body felt molten, hot enough to hurt. Its slick organs resisted her efforts to shove past them.

Alondra closed her eyes, visualizing the anatomy she'd studied. As his lungs inflated, his diaphragm thrust her hand back. The skin knitted together as soon as her fingertips slipped out of the wound.

Sweat beaded across her forehead. Alondra couldn't wipe her face with her bloody hands.

She made a third incision, cutting the diaphragm this time, wedging her hand deeper into Simon's chest. The pressure, as his body fought to expel her, was immense. She whimpered, forcing her way in. Everything around her hand throbbed in time with Simon's heartbeat. She wrapped her fingers around his heart, feeling for its arteries and veins.

The wound struggled to close around her wrist. Her bones ground together. She panicked, fearing his body would seal her hand inside until her spell wore off and he woke. That would be tricky to explain, she thought crazily. She carved an awkward opening and wrenched her hand free.

To do the job, she needed both hands up inside his body: one to hold the blade, the other to locate the blood vessels. Then she needed a third hand to keep the severed vessels from reconnecting as she moved around the heart. And a fourth hand to keep the chest incision from trapping her inside.

There was no way to do this alone, unless she found a way to kill Simon first, a way that kept his body from regenerating itself.

Maybe a log from the fire would cauterize the edges of the wound. Maybe if she filleted his body as she cut her way in. Maybe if she slashed her own wrists and contaminated his blood with her own. Maybe if she cut off his head…

She watched Simon heal one more time. She realized finally and without question that she had no right to kill him. Anybody who clung to life as tenaciously as Simon did had more claim to it than Victor, who'd made his peace with death. Since his first heart attack, the old man had been contentedly shrugging off life's hold.

And yet she had to have a heart for Victor. If he did not get a new heart, he would die. She had sworn that she would do anything in the world to save him. Now, faced with this, she could not keep her promise.

She'd never expected this adventure to prove challenging. Just slash the heart from Simon's body, plunk it in the enspelled cooler of dry ice, shower, and head to the airport. She was traveling anonymously on a good disposable passport; there was no way to connect this place and its contents to Victor. In and out fast, get Victor and the heart to the hospital, be on her way to a new life.

But fucking no.

The sleeping spell wouldn't last forever. Even if she let Simon up to walk away and count his blessings, she was fucked. He knew her name. He could track her down. And he lived for-fucking-ever.

Blood dripping from her fingertips, Alondra stood. What she wanted was something good and sturdy. Her bootlaces were probably not strong enough. Neither she nor Simon had worn belts. What about her scarf? Alondra fished it out of her coat pocket, leaving bloody smears on the white fur. Tugging the plum velvet between her hands, she looked up at the curtain rods, the light fixtures, and settled on the frame of the cupboard bed. The antique wood seemed solid.

It wasn't easy to loop the scarf over the wooden canopy. Still, she was determined. She gave thanks to her psychotic older brother for making sure she could tie a noose.

She shivered as the fire died back. She considered dressing, but she couldn't spare the time. Instead she shouldered naked into her wolf fur and set the desk chair on the bed. She contemplated leaving a note, but what would she say: "Sorry, Victor. I failed. Love you"? He'd know that anyway.

She climbed onto the bed, mounted the chair. It swayed for a heart-stopping moment. She didn't want to fall now. What if she broke her leg?

Once she was certain she had her balance, she slipped the noose over her head and kicked the chair away.

When she came to, Simon had run her a bath. He'd dressed, but his hair looked damp. He sat on the commode, blotting blood from his fur coat. "Welcome back."

"Why did you cut me down?" Alondra rasped.

"Because I like you."

"I like you, too."

Working patiently over the bloodstains, he let her cry. Despite herself, she couldn't help but be fascinated by someone as phlegmatic as Simon.

When her crying wound down, he asked, "Is that why you spared me? Because you like me?"

"Would it make what I've done any less horrific?"

"It would be more charming."

"Sorry, then. I lost my nerve."

"Points for honesty." He hung his coat over the bathroom door. "Let's get you out of that tub before you catch a chill."

Alondra held out her hands. Simon steadied her as she stepped out of the claw-footed tub. She huddled into the towel he draped around her.

He'd built the fire up again. The bedding wasn't too much of a shock as Simon tucked her inside.

"Join me?" Alondra asked.

Again Simon undressed with his back to her. Alondra scooted over to make room for him.

"No tears," he admonished. "I've forgiven you."

"Okay," Alondra promised hoarsely.

"What were you trying to do?"

She told him about Victor, how he'd protected her, what he meant to the world. She told Simon about the old man's need for a new heart.

Simon stroked red hair from her face. "In the morning, go back to him—"

"In London," she supplied.

"I will bring your old man a new heart."

Hope surged through Alondra, before reality clamped down. "I can't ask you to do that."

"I am here to kill a man. As I killed his uncle and his uncle before him, going back three centuries. I am their nemesis. Let this man's death serve some purpose beyond fulfilling an ancient curse."

It was wrong. Alondra knew it was wrong. Still, she agreed. "That black case over by the door…that's to transport the heart. It has spells on it that will shield it from curiosity and keep the heart fresh until it can be given to Victor." She snuggled against Simon, luxuriating in the heat his body gave off. "What can I pay you for this?"

"Nothing," Simon said, followed with a kiss. He leaned back to gaze into Alondra's eyes. "You know what I am and you're not afraid. That's rare and wonderful. It's enough for me."

She wondered if there'd be more to pay later, but she was committed now.

The Arms Dealer's Daughter

Ariel Shaad opened her eyes, eager to leap out of bed and see what the day would bring. Today she was twelve, legally an adult on Callixtos, and she could go where she liked. Her family had nothing more to say about it.

Her clock flashed with a message. When she pushed the button, her father's voice said, "Your gift is in the spare room. Happy birthday, Angel."

Ariel shrugged on a robe as she moved toward her door. She knew he'd had the servants rearranging things in the spare room. What could need a whole room? She hoped for a jet bike.

She slapped her hand on the palm lock. When the spare room's door opened, the room had been made over into a bedroom. On the narrow bed sat a small black-haired girl, dressed in an outgrown gray jumpsuit of Ariel's. The girl looked all of nine or ten, black eyes almost too large for her oval face. A ridged plastic collar ringed her neck and flowed over her collarbone.

Crushed, Ariel let the door close and went back to her own room to cry. She was too old to play with dolls, no matter how well-crafted.

Ariel flopped onto her bed and switched on the projection of dawn on the beach at Anchorhead. She and her mother had gone there on holiday a couple of months ago, but Ariel hadn't been able to persuade her parents that they needed a vacation home there. Not safe, her parents had decreed.

She sighed. It wasn't that she never got what she wanted. She looked at the wall decorated with her collection of alien sidearms. She'd bought them all over the galaxy, when she traveled with her father on sales calls. It was that her parents treated her like a child. The gift of a doll insulted her. She was twelve now and twelve meant adult. She wanted her freedom, not a new toy.

Her father sought Ariel in her room when he came home for lunch. "Don't you like her?"

"I'm not a little girl, Daddy. I don't want a doll."

"She's not a doll," he argued. "She's a bodyguard." He put a remote control unit into Ariel's hand. "I'm guaranteed that she's fully trained, but if she ever gives you a moment's concern, use this. She's wearing a shock collar. It will switch her off completely."

"I don't care how well it's trained," Ariel sulked. "I don't want a doll."

Her father bent down to kiss the top of her head. "I don't care what you want, Angel. On this planet, you're old enough to go where you like now. You will take your bodyguard with you everywhere you go, or I will have you ruled incapable and I will lock you in. Callixtos isn't a safe place and you know it."

Ariel stared at him, furious, but the clench of his jaw told her he wasn't going to give in. Grudgingly, she nodded.

"Good. She's called Rainy, but you can change that if you don't like it. Let's go visit her, so you can see how the remote works."

Ariel opened the spare room's door again. The doll sat on the edge of the bed once more. Its long straight black hair was mussed, as if by sleep.

"Speak to her," Daddy directed, "so she learns to recognize your voice."

"My father told me that you're my bodyguard," Ariel said. "He said I can leave the villa only if I take you with me. He says that you have to do what I say or I can use this." She held out the remote.

The doll's eyes widened. Clearly, it recognized the controller, understood what it could do. It didn't protest as Ariel pushed the button—and didn't make a noise as convulsions racked its body.

It was awful to watch. The doll looked like an insect thrown onto its back, limbs flailing. Breath huffed from it in ragged bursts. Foam flecked its lips.

Ariel felt her lunch lurch in her stomach. She wished for a way to make the punishment stop, but the control box only had the single button. She wondered if pressing it again would turn the convulsions off or double their duration. She looked to her father for help, but he watched the doll. Avidly.

Ariel shuddered. She'd take the remote to Feliss, see if he could wire in an off-switch.

The convulsions tapered off eventually. Ariel sat beside the doll, stroked its warm silken hair back from its face. It felt slightly damp to her touch, as if sweaty from the exertion. Ariel marveled at its realism. She wondered how much her father had paid for it.

"I'll leave you two to get acquainted," her father said. "I have to get back to the factory. She'll need to rest for a while, but then you can take her around the villa. Get used to her."

"Thank you, Daddy," Ariel said, more contritely.

"Of course, Angel."

After he left, Ariel examined the doll's hands, which were callused and lightly scarred. The short nails looked bitten to the quick. Long muscles roped the arms. Ariel ran her fingertips over the fringe of the doll's black eyelashes. A scar ran between its eyes. Did that mean the doll was secondhand? Or had it been scarred at the factory, to individualize it? Ariel wondered if it had been modeled on a real person, somebody's daughter. She wondered how old the original model was now.

Once its systems rebooted, the doll's eyes came open. It gazed at Ariel, its expression blank.

"Let's go down to the shop," Ariel said. "I want to see you shoot." She put the remote into the pocket of her pullover and walked over to unlock the door.

The doll followed her. It moved with startling fluidity. Ariel wondered if it was Templar tech; no other way to explain how it had been so cunningly made. Why would the Templars make human dolls, though?

Her dad's employees opened the range for them. Once she

got Rainy armored up, Ariel positioned the doll in front of the monitor with a command to "Watch." Then, flipping her visor down, Ariel took this year's Stinger pistol off the rack and stepped onto the range.

The simulation showed a three-dimensional cityscape, based on the neighborhood outside her family's villa, populated with robbers and beggars, kidnappers and addicts and people simply spoiling for a fight. Few of the simulations were human, so they wielded different sorts of weaponry and attacked at differing speeds. Ariel played through the course methodically, bored with its familiarity. She'd trained on it since she was old enough to hold a gun steady.

Once she'd finished, Ariel handed the Stinger to the doll. "Now you try."

Although the doll had never faced the course before, it got its shots off scary fast. As each simulated person popped up, Rainy shot them in the head, threat or not.

"You can't kill everyone," Ariel protested.

"I'm supposed to protect you," the doll argued. "I thought you wanted to know you'd be safe with me."

"I want to know you're not a psychopath," Ariel corrected. "Do it again. Just hit the threats."

So Rainy worked through the course again, still quick but now more accurately. It might let assailants get closer than Ariel would have, but it didn't shoot to wound.

Ariel wondered at the display inside the android's head. How much detail did it see? How did it calculate angles of attack? Were animations overlaid on the street scene or did it see in infrared, vapor trails, heat signatures?

Ariel bumped the range up in difficulty and sent Rainy through it again. Two salesgirls came to watch.

"Friend of yours?" Chelle asked.

"Birthday present." Ariel wondered if Rainy was a prototype, if her father intended to manufacture them in addition to the full line of hand weapons his factory made now. Would the bodyguards always look like ten-year-old girls or could the CPU be plunked into any human-sized form? A small girl had the advantage of looking non-threatening until you unleashed it, but there was a lot to be said for a sizeable deterrent.

Rainy finished the course for the third time and came to stand before Ariel. "This armor is hot," it complained. "Can I take it off?"

Ariel didn't want to wreck her new toy. She turned to Chelle. "Can it do the course without armor?"

"The lasers can blind her. If she takes a strike on bare skin, it will burn."

"Let me try," Rainy protested. "It's no fun in this turtle suit."

Ariel laughed. "Keep the helmet on," she ordered. "Your eyes are probably the most expensive part of you to replace."

Before dinner, Michette called to invite Ariel out for a drink. "It's your birthday," her friend reminded. "We *have* to celebrate." Michette named a bar near the mall, a place they'd been before where the music was loud and the drinks sweet. "Do you need us to come pick you up?"

"No," Ariel said. "I'll meet you there."

She dug through her wardrobe, looking for party clothes. She wanted to find something for Rainy to wear, too. Dress it up a little. Ariel was tall enough that one of her blouses could probably serve as a tunic on Rainy.

Her mother tapped on her door, then spoke through the comm. "I know Daddy gave you the big part of your present already, but I have something for you, too."

When Ariel unlocked her door, her mother asked, "Going out tonight?"

"Michette invited me to Amanita to celebrate."

"I suspected she would." Madame Shaad stepped aside so that her maid could hang something on the wardrobe's door. It was a tabard inset with gold, loops and whorls and curlicues of it. The metal smoldered like banked embers, slightly darker than Ariel's hair.

Ariel pulled the armor over her head to check its fit. The tabard covered her from collarbone to mid-thigh, slit so it wouldn't interfere with her pistol holster. "Oh, it's lovely," Ariel said. "And so light! Thank you."

"You must be outgrowing your old armor," her mother said.

"Your friend Michette's mother made this especially for you."

"It's perfect," Ariel said. "I can't wait to show it off tonight."

Her mother swept her up in a hug. "I can't believe you're so grownup already."

Ariel laughed. She felt like she had been waiting for this night forever.

Amanita was a glorified dancehall. It got around hiring waitstaff by installing drink dispensers. Usually people stood around the margins to drink, chucked their bottles into the cycler, then danced. The music was too loud for talking.

The club didn't restrict its clientele to any one species, so a spectrum of Callixtos's young people packed it. Anyone who bought a membership was welcome. The key was to arrive early. Either you got in before the club filled, or you went elsewhere. It wasn't safe to wait outside on the street.

As Ariel wove through the drinkers, Rainy stuck close on her left, so not to obstruct Ariel's gun hand. The doll's head tracked smoothly, scanning for threats.

Ariel's mouth felt uncomfortably dry. She'd never been out alone before. Usually she traveled between a pair of her father's guards, two big men called Gault and Schaefer. Gault had driven them to the club, but now he lingered near the door, as Ariel had ordered. He was close enough to help, but she couldn't duck behind him, if she needed to. For that matter, she couldn't duck behind Rainy either. The top of the doll's head barely cleared Ariel's collarbone.

Standing before the dispenser, Ariel realized that freedom made her anxious. She was glad the doll watched the room while she fumbled her credit chit from the pouch on her gun belt.

Ariel asked, "Need anything?"

Rainy made more of an expression than Ariel had seen yet, a good approximation of surprise. "Just water, please."

Ariel shrugged. She paid for synthemesc and water.

As Ariel turned, her hands filled with bottles, Feliss swooped out of the shadows. Before anyone could speak, Rainy had twisted one of his arms behind his back and forced him to the floor. People nearby laughed.

"Hey!" Ariel protested.

"Friend of yours?" As soon as Rainy registered Ariel's infinitesimal nod, it stepped back and pulled Feliss to his feet. He stood taller than the doll, taller than Ariel, with a lovely fan of cobalt blue hair that added another dozen centimeters of height. He was a year older than Ariel.

She flushed, embarrassed, and handed the bottled drinks to Rainy so she could hug Feliss. "Are you all right?"

He pecked her cheek. "Did you get a bodyguard for your birthday?"

"Yeah. Gault is around here somewhere, too, but Rainy's new. Glitchy, I guess. Sorry."

Feliss rubbed the back of his neck, where Rainy's hand had been. "Are they all like that when they're new?"

Ariel didn't know. She changed the subject. "Want a drink?"

"That's what I came to tell you. Michette reserved a back room. We have our own dispenser."

"That sounds like trouble." Ariel cracked the seal on her bottle and drank deeply as she followed Feliss through the club. A flavor like mangoes lingered on her tongue.

The back rooms at Amanita were geared for groups who wanted to do something more intimate than dance. Sinuous black upholstered couches circled a central padded space that could be used as a mattress. The dimly lit rooms didn't require decoration. Twinkling, bubbling lights adorned the ornate drink dispensers and music machines. If you wanted more light than that, you brought your own.

The back room Michette had reserved seemed barely large enough for everyone. Ariel's friends sprawled across the leather-sheathed furniture. "Happy birthday!" Michette shouted. Everyone sat up and switched on their sparklers, spelling inappropriate suggestions in the shadowy air. Ariel laughed, pleased to be the excuse for the party.

The room wouldn't have been so cramped, but as Ariel's eyes adjusted, she saw the bodyguards lining the walls. Most of them she recognized. Her closest friends were heirs and heiresses like she was, scions of families who custom-built racer ships or owned malls or mined asteroids or, in Michette's mother's case, designed bespoke personal armor. A scant handful of her friends were working people. Feliss repaired small machinery in a shop in the mall. Marcot sold Velocity and other chemicals, as required. Cam wrote intimate stories to order. They didn't have money to drink in a place like this, but they were fun, so they were always welcome to tag along.

"I didn't know you had a sister." Marcot slipped a little packet into Ariel's hand. She tucked the Velocity into her gun belt.

"Bodyguard," Ariel answered offhandedly. "Rainy, go stand with the other guards."

The doll went without complaint. All the other guards stood at least twice her height. None of the rest was human.

"Really?" Michette asked archly, amused. She was Gatinka, black-furred and vaguely feline. Tonight she wore a pinnacle of her mother's armor, adorned with fantastic birds. "That's your new guard?"

"I know." Ariel shook her head over the size discrepancy. "Isn't it hilarious?"

"I hope she'll grow," Marcot teased. Ariel laughed. She suspected he wished he had muscles like Rainy's.

"I sent it through the range this afternoon. Its aim is good." Ariel shrugged. "Ask Feliss how quickly it put him on the floor out in the club."

"Where'd she train?" Zenaida was Varan, a tall slim lizard who wore a lightweight version of Michette's mother's armor. Zenaida's mom owned a series of dojos, where all the kids had taken defense lessons when they were little.

"Don't know," Ariel answered. "My dad gave it to me this morning. He bought it somewhere."

"I wondered," Feliss said, "when I saw the collar."

"I wanted to ask you about that." Ariel pulled the remote out of her shoulder harness. Feliss took it gingerly in his obsessively manicured hands.

"The button sends Rainy into convulsions," Ariel said. "Mean, ugly, mouth-foaming convulsions. Is there a way to add an off-switch to the control?"

"What are you asking me for?"

"A way to stop the convulsions after they begin? So they don't go on as long."

Feliss looked at her from under his cobalt blue bangs. "Just don't push the button."

Ariel wondered if the synthemesc garbled her speech. "My dad said to use the controller to keep it in line." She enunciated her Galactic Standard carefully. It wasn't her first language, but she was fluent. "When I tested the remote this afternoon, it was horrible to watch. I actually felt sorry for Rainy. I don't want it to suffer. I just want it to obey."

Feliss stared at her. "I didn't think you were as bad as the rest of them, Ariel."

She frowned. "The synthemesc is affecting me. You're not making sense. Can I bring Rainy and the remote by your shop tomorrow? So you can fix it?"

Feliss nodded unhappily. He handed the remote back as if glad to be rid of it. "I'll help if I can."

He turned his back to talk to Cam. Ariel couldn't figure out how she'd offended him. She gulped the synthemesc to cover her self-consciousness.

The drug was definitely taking effect. The music reverberated in her ears. Rainbows in a spectrum of blue ringed the lights of the music machine. Ariel had another sip of synthemesc.

An enormous boom shuddered through the room. The explosion made the walls flex. The music fell silent as the lights struggled, then went out.

Beyond the soundproofing, distant screams echoed through the club outside.

Ariel's friends huddled together, drawing their sparklers for comfort. Ariel set down the last of her synthemesc to free up her gun-hand.

The bodyguards switched on torches. Their beams crisscrossed the room as they located their wards.

Rainy appeared at Ariel's side, fastened a hand like a claw around Ariel's wrist, and pulled her away from the crowd. It stepped up onto a sofa. "We're going this way." It nodded up at the ventilation hatch. "Give me a boost?"

Ariel bent one knee and gave the doll a hand for balance as it stepped up onto her thigh. Rainy sprang upward toward the vent cover, punching it open as it jumped. It caught the edge of the hatch with its other hand, then hauled itself upward to look inside the duct.

Satisfied, the doll slithered up through the hatch. Ariel wondered if it was ditching her. She switched off the sparkler, ready to drop it and pull out the remote, but Rainy bent downward through the hole to offer its hands. "Jump up," it encouraged.

One of the bodyguards announced, "The back door's blocked. We're gonna have to blow it out."

Ariel looked skeptically at the android overhead. She wasn't sure she could jump high enough to catch its hands, to say nothing of pulling herself through the hatch.

"Go." Feliss stepped up onto the sofa behind Ariel. He put his hands around her waist and added his strength behind her jump. Rainy caught Ariel's hands and hauled her upward. Ariel clambered over the doll into the dusty duct.

"Get Feliss, too," she ordered. Rainy leaned back through the hatch and hauled the tinker up enough that he could crawl over her also.

When the three of them sat inside the duct, catching their breaths, the chaos out in the main club was easier to hear. Ariel recognized small arms fire: Stinger pistols, probably wielded by security guards.

"What do we do now?" Ariel begged.

"Get you home," Rainy said. "Follow me. Keep quiet."

"What's going on?" Ariel asked.

Rainy shrugged. "Does it matter? The party's over."

"My friends are down there."

"Their guards are too big to get up here with us and I can't protect all your friends by myself," the doll reasoned. "Let's go."

Ariel looked down through the hatch. A hand grabbed her gun belt. She prepared to fight, but Rainy didn't try to drag her back. It simply held her, so Ariel wouldn't fall.

Ariel leaned back through the hole. Down below, Michette

and the others had collected in a corner, shielded by a couple of their bodyguards while the others prepared to open the back door with explosives.

Big Michette probably couldn't wedge herself through the hatch. Zenaida could've fit, but she wouldn't run from a fight. Ariel's human friends huddled too far away to hear her calling their names over the increasing chaos in the outer club.

"I smell smoke," Feliss said.

"We need to go," Rainy repeated. "If you ever want to leave the villa again, Ariel, you need to prove to your dad that you can get home safely."

Ariel shook her head mutely. The synthemesc flickered in her vision, unnerving now instead of fun.

"Come on." Feliss offered his hand. "You know their guards are top-flight. How many scrapes have you all gotten out of together? Call them in the morning and trade stories of your escapes."

Ariel let him pull her along. With his free hand, he ignited his sparkler and handed it up to Rainy. The doll nodded thanks and started crawling at a good clip. Ariel lit her own sparkler so they could follow.

They hadn't gone very far when Ariel ordered, "Stop. I need to take my armor off. I keep crawling on it."

The others waited as she struggled out of the tabard. Ariel rolled it up, then secured it across her back with the strap of her shoulder harness. "That's better."

Rainy led them through the ventilation system as if it knew where it was going. Ariel couldn't figure out how it navigated. Could it access schematics of every building in town? Did it see air currents? Whatever it was, the android brought them to a vent that led to the outside. A rotary fan turned lazily across its mouth. Rainy kicked the fan, hard, but it didn't give.

"Let me," Feliss offered. He unrolled the tools he always carried in the back pocket of his jacket and set to work dismantling the fan.

"Will your parents worry?" Rainy asked. "You should call, let them know we'll be on our way home soon."

"They're probably asleep," Ariel hoped. "I don't want to

wake them. I'll call Gault, though. Maybe he can meet us with the truck."

She keyed him up on her bracelet. The call went unanswered. Last she'd seen him, he had been loitering near the club's entrance, gossiping with the other guards. She wondered if he was fighting his way to the back room, where her friends awaited rescue. He'd be angry when he got in there and she'd vanished. She left him a message, so he wouldn't worry, and promised to meet him at the truck.

Rainy helped Feliss push the rotary fan aside. Then the doll slipped out through the vent. "We're in an alley," it reported. "Stay where you are. I'll see what's going on at the street."

Feliss watched it go.

Ariel asked, "It's really well made, isn't it? You wouldn't know it wasn't human."

His head jerked toward Ariel sharply. She would have read his expression as a frown, but that didn't make sense.

"Where did she come from?" he asked quietly.

Ariel shrugged. "My dad has been sneaking around all week. He's had the servants clearing out the spare room. It's all set up like a bedroom for Rainy now. I'm not sure why he went to all that trouble, when a closet would've done. Do you think it needs to lie down when it switches off?"

"You really don't know, do you?" Feliss asked.

Rainy preempted her reply. "We can't go out that way. Can you climb?"

Ariel looked down at the flimsy party shoes she'd worn. "If I have to," she said doubtfully.

The alley walls were faced with native stone. Rainy climbed by wedging its fingers between the stones. It scrambled up to the building's fire slide, pulled the pin, and let the last story down.

Ariel took off her shoes and buckled them over the back of her gun belt. Feliss followed her lead and stripped off his boots and socks. Then they followed Rainy up and up and up the pipe of the fire escape.

The synthemesc fluttered blackly around the edges of Ariel's vision. She tried not to think about whether Amanita was on fire behind them or who the target of tonight's raid had been. She tried not to worry about her friends trapped in the back room. Her bracelet hadn't buzzed once. No one called to make sure she was all right, not even Gault.

Tears rolled down her cheeks, but she kept pushing herself up the fire slide.

"Who's dripping on me?" Feliss asked.

"Sorry." Ariel sniffled. "This isn't how I planned to spend my birthday."

He chuckled gently. "I'm sorry about that. Good thing you brought Rainy along tonight."

"I guess so. How much farther do we have to climb?"

"We're almost to the roof," Rainy reported. "We'll slide down on the other side of the building."

Once they finally reached the rooftop, Rainy insisted Ariel put her armor back on. Then it led them across the roof and asked them to crouch down as it scanned for problems. Ariel had gotten all turned around, but she thought they must be a block away from the garage where Gault always parked the truck.

"What kind of trouble are you kids up to?" a voice demanded.

Ariel flopped over onto her back, hands out away from her gun. Two of the building's security team stood over them, guns drawn. Ariel couldn't see if their weapons had been set to stun.

"There was an attack on Amanita." Ariel's voice quavered. "We're just trying to get home."

The guards wore ill-fitting torso shields and cheap vacu-formed helmets. "Yeah? You sure you didn't just trespass up here so you'd have a place to make out under the stars?"

Not a bad idea, Ariel had to admit. It hadn't even occurred to her. "I'm sorry about the trespassing," she said. "We were scared. We just ran."

"We'll detain you until we get hold of your next of kin," the other guard threatened. He nodded at her armor. "You look like you'd be worth something to someone."

It wouldn't be the first time Ariel was ransomed to her parents, but she hadn't wanted it to happen again, especially not on her first night out alone.

Sniper fire crackled from one of the rooftops behind the guards. They glanced around to see if they should take cover.

In the momentary distraction, Rainy launched herself at the security team. They stood taller than she did, but she was moving fast. She kicked one in the face screen hard enough to rattle his display. Then she grabbed hold of the other's arm, forcing the muzzle of his gun downward until she broke his wrist.

Feliss caught Ariel's hand and pulled her into the fire slide on the far side of the building.

Rainy joined them on the last landing above the street. "Everything okay?" Ariel asked.

"Sure." Rainy's cheeks seemed pinked by the exercise, but it didn't look damaged. "Ready to run for the parking garage?"

When they reached the truck, Gault wasn't there. Ariel touched her bracelet to the vehicle, which unlocked obligingly. "What do we do now?" she asked. Exhaustion had amplified the last effects of the synthemesc so that everything around her throbbed with the rattle of her heart. She felt shaky, close to tears again.

"Can you drive?" Rainy asked Feliss.

"Never had enough money to learn," he said. "You?"

"I could probably figure it out, but I don't think I can reach the controls." In fact, she was so little that she had to reach up to the door handle.

"I can do it," Ariel promised. "I'm not that messed up."

"Then drive us home." The android went around to the passenger side and climbed in. "Give me your gun. I'll clear us a path, if I need to."

Ariel handed over her Stinger, a prototype for next year's guns. Rainy checked its charge and thumbed it live.

Turning to Feliss, Ariel begged, "Come with me. I'll run you home in the morning. I just want off the street now. And I don't want you wandering around out here alone."

He checked his chrono, then piled into the truck's cab to share Rainy's seat. "I need to open the shop at 08 tomorrow."

"I promise I'll get you there on time."

Ariel started the truck's engine and eased out of the parking garage. With the synthemesc overlaying her vision like an oil slick, swirling with ribbons of green and lavender, she drove more cautiously than normal.

Ariel parked the truck inside the villa and took a long, quavering breath. "No one's called all night," she said.

"You haven't called them, either," Feliss reminded. "Why don't you try Michette now?"

"It's late," Rainy pointed out.

"They'll still be up," Feliss argued. "It's not like they need to go to work tomorrow." Ariel wondered if she heard bitterness in his voice. She'd never cared that Feliss had a job. She'd done what she could to bring him her family's appliances to mend, tipping well because he always did such meticulous repairs.

Hurt by his remark, she countered, "I need to work tomorrow."

"In your dad's shop?" Feliss prodded.

"Yeah."

"Flirting with customers and showing off on the gun range?"

"Yeah? Just because he doesn't pay me doesn't mean it isn't work," Ariel protested.

Feliss tried to catch Rainy's eye, but the doll was searching the courtyard's rooftops, noting the family guards. One nodded to it.

"We should go in," Rainy said. "It's been a long night."

"You need to get some sleep," Ariel told Feliss.

He nodded, offering her a smile as if he'd forgiven her. "Your parents have a guest room?"

"Several," Ariel said. "You can take your pick."

When Ariel led the others into the villa, her parents sat in the parlor, waiting for her. "Thank goodness," her mother said, promptly bursting into tears.

Ariel looked to her dad for explanation.

"We heard from Gault that there had been an attack at that club you like. Then his comm went offline. The news said there was a firebombing. Snipers were shooting people down in the street as they evacuated the club."

"We thought the worst," her mother sobbed. "Oh, Ariel, why didn't you call?"

"Rainy said I should, but I thought you'd be asleep," Ariel snapped. "I don't know what happened to Gault, but I haven't been able to reach him either. I was never in any danger, though. Rainy got us out of the club safely and I drove the truck home."

An awkward silence fell. Ariel realized they stared over her shoulder. "This is my friend Feliss," she said. "You've met him before. He works at the repair shop in the mall."

That angered Ariel's mother enough to stop her crying.

"We're only friends," Ariel argued quickly, before her mother could start in. "I didn't want to drive him home tonight. I wanted to come straight back. I told him he could have one of the guest rooms and I'd take him to work in the morning."

"I don't want to impose," Feliss said. "It was a pleasure to meet you both again."

"Don't be silly," Ariel told him. She turned back to her parents. "We are all adults here. If I wanted to sleep with Feliss, it's none of your business. But I don't. He's a friend and he needs a place to sleep tonight, so please don't embarrass him."

Ariel's dad took her mother's hand and patted it. "You're right, Angel. It's going to take some time for us to adjust to your new status. Why don't you show your friend to a room and let's all get some sleep. Business isn't going to do itself in the morning."

Ariel kissed her parents good night and led Feliss off toward the guest wing. Rainy trailed along silently.

Morning came far too early. Rainy stood at the side of Ariel's bed. "I'm sorry," it said. "Feliss needs to get to work."

"I'm up," Ariel groaned. "Find me some clothes." She waved toward the wardrobe. "Find yourself something to wear, too. We'll go buy you clothes, after Feliss rebuilds the remote."

While Rainy poked through the wardrobe, Ariel checked her messages. Michette had called sometime before dawn. "Hope you got home safely last night." A grin warmed the Gatinka girl's voice. "We had an adventure. The guards finally got the door open, but we had a firefight getting back to our truck. Cam got shot, but he'll be all right. I'm going to ask Mother to give him some armor. There must be something around here with a flaw in it, something she hasn't been able to sell. Oh, and Marcot took too much Velocity and said he was going to have a stroke. You humans are too delicate for life on Callixtos," Michette teased.

Switching the subject before Ariel could take offense, Michette asked, "Did I see you sneaking off with Feliss? Lucky girl. Hope you made his dreams come true." She giggled. "I need to take something and get some sleep. Call me at a decent hour and let me know where you want to go tonight."

Ariel answered, "I want to take Rainy to the mall. Meet me there?" She pressed send and turned to dress.

Rainy had gotten Feliss up first. When Ariel arrived at his guest room's door, he had showered and put on the previous night's party clothes.

"Come back in your room for a minute," she suggested.

"Your parents…"

Ariel cut him off. "Rainy can chaperone."

Once the door had closed, Ariel pulled out the packet of Velocity that Marcot had slipped her as a birthday present. "This won't make up for your lack of sleep," she said, "but it should help you get through the day."

"Just a little," Feliss said. "I've got to sit in the shop until 03."

Ariel poured lines out on the polished stone counter in the washroom and let Feliss go first.

"Come on in," Feliss said. Ariel had never seen him open the shop before. She stood out of the way as Rainy helped him push open the riot shutters. Then he switched on the lights and daytime security. Feliss's shop wasn't as big inside as Ariel's wardrobe, but tools lined three of its walls. It would be worth his life to have to replace them all.

Once he settled on his stool, Ariel pulled out the remote for Rainy's collar. "Last night, I was trying to ask if you could install an off-switch on this."

"I understood what you were asking." Feliss looked at her from under his bangs again. "She saved your ass last night."

"I know," Ariel argued. "That's why I want an off-switch on the remote. I want to be able to get Rainy's attention, shut it off if I need to, but I don't see why it needs to suffer."

Feliss shook his head. "Ariel, Rainy is…"

"Don't," Rainy interrupted, her voice tight, almost angry. "It's okay. Please."

Feliss gazed at it, ignoring Ariel altogether. Puzzled by his compassion for the android, Ariel felt a bit jealous. "Just tell me," she urged.

Rainy's head twitched no.

Feliss sighed. "All right. I'll let you tell her, whenever you're ready to."

"Thank you," the doll said.

Ariel frowned, staring from one to the other of them.

The Energizer Bunny at Home

Dawn blasted through the uncurtained living room window. It burned through my eyelids and shoved me awake. Moaning, I sat up and pushed the tangled hair out of my face. I'd only had an hour of sleep on Neal's sofa. I couldn't go on like this. Alan had to die today.

Tad, Alan's ex, sat at the dining room table, huddled over his Ouspensky book. He looked thinner, grayer in the morning light, shadows smudged under his hazel eyes. I sent him to nap on the sofa. He couldn't believe I was awake again already, but he'd been up all night long and didn't argue. As he settled down to sleep, I went in to check on Alan.

I watched carefully to make certain he was still breathing. I couldn't get used to his Auschwitz physique. His skin had the consistency of yellowed leather. It draped his collarbone and between each individual rib. During the night, his eyes had come halfway open. He could not have looked more like a corpse. *Enough with the dress rehearsal already.*

I pressed the button on the morphine pump, listened to the comforting whine as the computer measured out another dose. *Stay asleep,* I prayed. *Drift away.* I'd come back in ten minutes and give him another dose.

My friend Neal had talked to Alan the day before, during his husband's last period of awareness. "Let go," Neal encouraged. "It's okay for you to leave me. I don't want you to suffer any longer."

"I don't know how to let go," Alan argued, weak and furious. "Tell me how to die."

None of us living knew the answer. We did our best to keep him asleep after that. The doctor said we could give him Phenobarbitals when the morphine wasn't enough.

Lingering in the doorway, smelling the sweet rot of his

sickness, I considered holding a pillow over Alan's face. He was too weak to prevent me. He might struggle out of reflex, but he was only a skeleton. I probably had seventy pounds on him. He wanted to die. He said so repeatedly every lucid moment. Those of us nursing him needed a full night's sleep, needed steady meals, needed a lot less chocolate and coffee and anxiety in our systems. We needed this stress to be over. Otherwise, we would all get sick. We needed Alan to let go of life. How?

Pushing the morphine pump every ten minutes had been hard enough for me at first. I fully believe that everyone has a right to end his or her own life when living becomes intolerable for whatever reason. But as determined as Alan had been to do himself in—throughout the downhill course of his illness—he flinched when faced with the handfuls of pills required for oblivion. He thought the morphine pump would be his savior. One night's button-pushing party, he said, and he'd float away on a painless cloud.

That was five days ago. Since then, death had become a hands-on experience for me. Since we began giving him the morphine, Alan hadn't eaten a single bite of solid food. He was starving to death at our hands. At my hands.

After the first few days of false hope, I realized that none of us understood what the morphine was supposed to do. We expected it would keep Alan sedated enough to sleep. Alan hoped it would sedate him enough to die. Unfortunately, the computer measured out doses insufficient to do either.

Even when the hospice nurse upped Alan's dosage each day, nothing prevented him from waking to insist he never wanted to wake up again. Nobody argued. Still, his tolerance for the drug outstripped the poison building up in his emaciated body.

His sympathetic doctor admitted there was no hope for Alan's condition. Even though he had prescribed the copious amounts of morphine, he would not—could not—take the responsibility of administering the drug in a single dose. Where was Jack Kevorkian when we needed him?

I'd told Neal I would be there for him when the time came. When I made the promise, I expected "the time" to be overnight. Alan's death was stretching out toward a week. The alternative to

Kevorkian—amateur-assisted suicide—was looking more and more attractive. This nightmare was what we were reduced to when the doctor-assisted suicide mandate failed to get enough votes.

Ursula, Alan's cat, curled on the chair beside the morphine pump. She kept vigil when I could no longer stand to be in the room. I wished Ursula could learn to push the pump's button for me. Then someone who loved Alan would kill him.

I felt guilty about that thought. Truth was, I loved Neal. I thought of him as my younger brother. Alan, who had married into the "family" three years ago, had never tried to overcome my resistance to him. It didn't help that they'd gone down to City Hall to sign the Domestic Partner paperwork without asking for witnesses. I would have stood up for them, showered them with rose petals, thrown them a party. The commitment between these two lone wolves was a huge deal. They hadn't wanted anyone to fuss over it. I felt left out. In the end, I forced myself to believe it was enough that they loved each other. I didn't need to understand it to recognize it.

During the previous interminable night, smoking yet another joint in an attempt to find some appetite, Neal talked about why he'd married Alan. Neal had tested positive first, in May 1991. He wanted there to be someone who would take care of him as he died. Ironically, before Neal got sick, Alan caught a worse strain of the plague. *His* death raced out of nowhere with blinding speed.

Alan was only the first: that's all I could think. Next would be Neal. Then I'd lose the gay friend who took me to the senior prom. He'd been positive for two years. His husband had tested positive in the spring. From now on, I thought, I will always know someone who is dying. Once the first domino fell, there would be no stopping the cascade.

I wondered exactly how many other families were facing this same nightmare at this same ungodly hour of this beautiful Monday morning. How many people in San Francisco were clinging to the edge of life? How many in New York, LA, the US, across the world? Death was everywhere. Being one of many survivors made it worse. Everything made it worse.

I thought of Neal, sleeping with Seconal in the next room. He was 27, too young to be losing his husband, too young to be making cremation arrangements, too young to face his own looming illness. I would have cried, if I'd had the strength. It took all my strength to put my book down every ten minutes so I could give Alan more morphine.

I hated Alan for making this all so difficult. I wished he'd had the courage to take the responsibility he'd said he would. *Talk about blaming the victim.* I knew I was being unreasonable, but couldn't stop myself. There was too much time to think when you were awake twenty-three hours of every twenty-four.

I weighed the down pillow in my hands. Alan was so frail. It hurt to look at him, like a hammer between my eyes. *It would be a mercy*, I thought, *an act of kindness. And I never had to tell anyone what I'd done.*

I put the pillow back on the bed and pushed the morphine button. I couldn't kill Alan. I couldn't stop his breathing. I knew I would feel his life on my hands like something viscous. I wasn't killing him to free him. I wasn't killing him out of love. I would be killing him to save Neal, who might develop symptoms if this ordeal continued much longer. I would be killing Alan for my own sanity, killing him out of jealousy and anger and the selfish desire for a full night's uninterrupted sleep in my own bed. No matter how I argued with myself that it would ultimately be for the best, that it was only a matter of time anyway, I couldn't see killing Alan as a noble act. I didn't have the courage to do it alone.

By the time Darren arrived at 10, I skated along the thin ice of hysteria. He was a big, bluff bear with a carefully trimmed beard and a voice that often boomed too loud. I stopped him on the doorstep and closed the door behind me. In greeting I said, "He has to die today."

Darren nodded. He'd offered "to take the batteries out of the bunny" whenever Neal got ready.

I tried to convince Darren to do it immediately, while everyone else slept. That way, I hoped, it might look like a natural death and less like murder. If Alan were dead for a while before Neal got up, the responsibility and the decision would be lifted off his shoulders.

Darren calmed me down as well as he could. He didn't want to do anything without consulting Neal. He spoke from experience. In January, when Darren's own lover chose to opt out rather than suffer any longer, Neal fed him the pills that killed him. Eight months later, Darren was prepared to return the favor—but not without Neal's express permission. He went in to sit with Alan.

I was relieved to take a break from administering the morphine.

I should have gone home. Maybe I could have gotten a grip on myself. Instead, I took a shower, put on the clean clothes I'd brought, and tried to resign myself to another day. *This wasn't so bad*, I told myself. Neal and Alan had collected more music than I could exhaust in a month. They had plenty of books to read, lots of magazines to page through, several good jigsaw puzzles to pass the time. Only the television was off-limits, facing the bed in which Alan lay.

Tad ran out to retrieve some bagels for breakfast. He was eager for a walk in the fresh wind blowing off the bay. Later, there would be sailboats, white on the blue water. I would watch them skipping across the waves from the living room window.

I put "Miss Perfumado" into the disc player again. Would I ever be able to listen to Caesaria Evora's fabulous voice without thinking of Alan, shriveled and wheezing, marooned on the edge of agony? Would I ever have a life again, instead of someone else's death? I wasn't thinking coherently. I'd forgotten how.

When Neal finally wandered out of his room in his bathrobe, haggard face itching with brown stubble, he blinked back tears, disappointed that nothing had changed. I told him I'd considered the pillow option. Neal admitted he also had looked at the bedding as a lethal weapon. Tad confessed he had, as well.

Even though we were all agreed, Neal didn't want to do anything until the hospice nurse came.

Unfortunately, hours later, she couldn't promise anything. Alan's blood pressure hovered at 80/40, extremely low, but his feet were still warm. That meant his circulation had not yet begun to fail. He'd woken while she took his pulse and asked for a drink of water. He asked her, "How much longer is it going to take?" She told him honestly, she'd had other patients linger at this stage for almost a month. A month!

I couldn't get her out of the house fast enough.

Darren and I discussed what we needed to do.

Step One was to send Tad and Neal out to a movie. They had to be out of the house. I sent Tad out to buy a newspaper, so they could scan the possibilities. The movie needed to be big, loud, absorbing, and not obsessed with death. Their choices were *Speed, True Lies*, and *Clear and Present Danger. The Adventures of Priscilla, Queen of the Desert* and *Natural Born Killers*, both of which Alan would have loved, were coming soon. It was a choice I was glad not to have to make.

Step Two was to find a plastic bag. Darren admitted he was saving a Tower Records bag in a drawer by his bed for when his own time came.

I did not think ahead to Step Three. All I knew was that the bunny was going down if I had to take his batteries out myself. I opened the kitchen cabinet and began sorting through the plastic grocery bags.

Never Bargained for You

The shop sat on the less-fashionable end of Melrose, toward Paramount Studios, away from the Hollywood boutiques. Dust smeared its windows less as a decorative motif than as a philosophical statement. A mangy taxidermized chimpanzee crouched behind the glass. In its paw rested a human skull, spade marks still visible on the dirt-scuffed cranium. Secondhand books on ritual magic encircled the monkey. The masking tape on their covers quoted very low prices.

Jimmy swung open the door. The room held a memory of unpleasant incense. The gaunt proprietor gave him a smile that manipulated the ropy muscles of his face into a cadaver's grimace. *One step ahead of death*, Jimmy thought.

"Looking for anything particular?" The owner's voice was a wheeze with a French accent.

"Just want to browse the books, mate."

"As you will."

Jimmy was paging through Regardie's *The Eye in the Triangle*, wondering if he should spend the money, when she walked in. She didn't look like the rest of the Melrose Avenue hippie/stripper/cocktail waitresses, ludicrously leggy with boobs the size of cantaloupes. Instead, she was all curves that swooped gracefully from one part of her anatomy to the next. Watching her walk was like drinking bourbon while playing guitar and getting a blowjob. Saliva flooded Jimmy's mouth as he watched her weave between the little cases filled with amulets and trinkets.

As if she felt his gaze, she swiveled toward him. The front of her didn't disappoint. Her eyes glowed an unusual shade of purple. Staring into them, Jimmy lost the ability to think at all.

She smiled, all kinds of amused.

Then her attention focused on the proprietor. He'd come

around the counter to catch her up in a hug. That delicious body pressed against the cadaverous old man like she meant it.

Jimmy swallowed hard on his jealousy. The magickal text lay forgotten in his hands as he tried to figure out who she was, what she was doing here. He couldn't believe that anyone so breathtaking could be unknown in Hollywood. Even if she were only a call girl, someone would have decided she could make more money in movies. Even legitimate movies, where she kept her clothes on.

She and the owner whispered together, her head on his shoulder. Her hair was a shifting shade of brown—sometimes chestnut threaded with gold, sometimes nearly black with a red undertone—that tumbled in loose curls down her back. She wore a royal purple wrap dress that hugged her tight around the waist, then swirled to her knees. Black-seamed stockings ran razor-straight down to shoes he hoped she wore as a joke. The heel shafts were pistol barrels. Bright brass bullet casings lined up on end to form the platform for her toes.

Jimmy couldn't decode her relationship to the gnarly old geezer. He looked old enough to be her great-granddad—and by no means wealthy, judging from the dust and junk in the shop—but she cozied up to him like he was the center of her world.

A shadow fell across the shop's doorway. The girl turned toward it, which directed Jimmy's attention that way.

The guy standing there looked big enough to play for Chelsea. He wore a matte black suit over a black silk shirt and tie. The funereal clothing emphasized everything wrong with his face. Not just his nose had been broken, but every bone in his face looked askew.

The shop reverberated with the sound of the girl's heels sauntering across the worn linoleum. She slid into the long black car at the curb without a backward glance.

"Help you?" the owner rasped in a voice like a dead bug.

Speaking more truthfully than intended, Jimmy blurted, "I want one o' those."

The old man chuckled lasciviously. "Doesn't everyone?" He disappeared through the moth-eaten curtain behind the register.

Jimmy listened to him rummaging around back there. He

looked down at the Regardie book, but its appeal had evaporated. He checked his watch. He should be getting back, getting ready for the show.

"Look at this," the old guy wheezed, reverently setting another book on the counter. A scar ran across its black-leather cover. "This is what you need to get a girl like Lorelei."

Lorelei, Jimmy repeated to himself. He ran his hand over the book. Did he imagine that it was cold to the touch? He split it open to a random page, found a meticulous woodcut of a magic circle. The paper looked *ancient*. "How much?"

The old man grinned, revealing teeth stained yellow as dandelions. "Eighty-seven bucks and that watch."

Jimmy pulled the money from his pocket. He counted it out, surprised to find eighty-seven American dollars. He stripped the watch off and laid it on the counter, too. It had been a gift from his mum.

The owner wrapped the book in brown paper, tied it with string. It looked like a packet from the butcher's when he finished. "Glad to help a fellow seeker," he said.

After the door closed behind him, Jimmy realized he no longer had cab fare. He'd have to walk back to the Chateau Marmont. He ripped the wrapping off the book and pitched it into the first trash bin he passed.

As he strolled along, devouring the text, he found his steps taking on a certain rhythm. He heard music in his head: heavy, wailing guitars. He was new to magic, but music he felt in his blood.

The music made sense of the arcane directions of the ritual, which were full of implements and ingredients he would never have time to acquire. The band was only in LA for another couple of days, before the bus carried them off on their first US tour.

He had to have her. Now, before they left LA.

Lorelei, his thoughts crooned. *What kind of name was Lorelei? Had her parents named her that, or was it a stage name? Did she dance somewhere?* His body reacted warmly to the thought of Lorelei gyrating on a stage.

He closed the book, held it low across his hips like a guitar.

The weight of the book as he walked was very pleasurable.

The crowd outside the Whisky a Go Go had spilled off the sidewalk onto Sunset Boulevard. Lorelei asked the driver to drop her off a block away so she could walk up. The night was unseasonably warm for January, which put everyone in a good mood. She wanted to savor that.

Lorelei slipped into a shadow and changed her dress. The purple wraparound had suited her afternoon business, but now she needed something funkier. She opted for a halter-top slip, still purple, with a short handkerchief hem. Its swooping neckline revealed more skin than she usually did. This was no time to be subtle.

She kept the pistol-heeled shoes, though. They were her new favorites.

As she stalked up to the velvet rope, her gaze sought the bouncer's. He inclined his head toward the door. Lorelei ambled past the line, giving him her best smile. His sigh caught the attention of the other girls in line.

The band was taking the stage as she came in. Lorelei headed over to get a drink. When the boys launched into their first song, the crowd surged toward them, galvanized immediately into dancing. Lorelei found herself alone with the bartender. She ordered a Harvey Wallbanger and leaned back to watch the show.

Jimmy looked up from his guitar. The music felt really good tonight, every molecule of him in tune and singing. He wanted to see if the crowd felt it.

Out beyond the stage lights, they were mostly faceless shadows. He watched them dancing to the music, on the beat, in sync. He glanced over at Bobby, on fire tonight, shrieking his lungs out.

Bobby had fixated on someone out in the audience. Generally, that meant some spectacularly pretty girl.

Jimmy checked his guitar cord, making sure he hadn't gotten tangled in Jonesy's bass cord. He prowled across the tiny stage. He stepped into the spotlight long enough to feel its heat, then moved back, triangulating.

There was a blank spot in the crowd. People had backed away from someone. Jimmy could hardly believe his luck. There she was: Lorelei.

She danced like a flame flickering in time to the music. He marveled that she didn't wriggle out of her dress, just a slip of a thing after the demure wraparound this afternoon.

The song crescendoed and crashed to a stop. Lorelei flung her hair back from her face, catching her breath.

Jonesy's bass strode into the next song, ponderous and stately. Lorelei found the rhythm and writhed.

Jimmy brought his guitar in, weaving around the bass line, but his mind was no longer focused solely on the music.

Lorelei put her hands under her hair, raised it off her back. Jimmy imagined her doing that above him, hips riding him in that same slow rhythm…

Bobby missed his cue. Jimmy's attention snapped back to the stage. His fingers followed Jonesy's bass, leading up to the verse again.

Bobby bent over the end of the stage, shouting into Peter's ear.

Dammit. The singer had poached Jimmy's girl. In a rage, Jimmy watched Peter wind through the crowd toward Lorelei.

Then the first of the onlookers put his hand on Lorelei. He caught her shoulder, tried to turn her toward him. Another man shoved the first away. Then there were fists flying—and Peter, fearless as ever, diving into the fray.

He guided Lorelei free. Time stopped for an instant as Lorelei looked up at the stage. She ignored Bobby, Bonzo, Jonesy, the whole room full of people. Her eyes met Jimmy's— and she smiled.

He knew then that all his dreams were going to come true.

Lorelei followed the tour manager backstage, but she'd been there so often, she could've found her own way.

"You tryin' to start a fight out there?" he growled, menacing enough.

"I was just dancing," she purred.

Once he'd unlocked the dressing room, he held the door open for her. As she passed by, she turned her head to trail her hair across his arm. She watched him consider asking for a private show, but duty—or the itch for a fight—overcame his lust.

"You wait here," he ordered. "I need to check on the lads."

Lorelei heard the bolt shoot as he locked her in. As if she might run away.

She pulled a rickety spindle-backed chair under the monitor, stepped up onto the seat, and stretched to turn the sound on. At least she could listen to the show.

She prowled the room, hoping for something to drink. Beer bottles sank into a dishpan full of melting ice. She popped the cap off one with the back of the chair and drank deep.

The band was amazing. Hearing the crowd react to them, well, she wouldn't need to promise fame and fortune. Those were clearly just a matter of time.

What, then? Girls seemed in easy supply. Drugs weren't a bargaining point, judging from the roaches crushed amongst the cigarette butts in the ashtray. Talent, beauty, youth: none of those were lacking. What was it Jimmy wanted?

Her? She'd taken exclusive contracts in years past, but recently she'd just drifted from mark to mark, collecting souls as she went. Might be nice to settle down—if by settling down, you meant going on tour with a guitarist destined for greatness and his sex-god lead singer, both muse and adversary. Sounded like fun.

Lorelei examined the guitar cases. The second one she opened held Daniel's book. Lorelei grinned, hefting the *Ars Magica Arteficii*. She sank into the shaky chair, propped her heels on the equally rickety card table—so that anyone coming through the door would get the best look at her legs—and began to read.

After the show ended with two encores, she heard the boys coming backstage in a maelstrom of testosterone and adrenaline. *Showtime.*

A key fumbled in the lock before the door swung open. Four sweaty boys tumbled in.

Closing the *Ars Magica*, Lorelei looked them over coolly. The decibel level dropped instantly.

"What," she drawled, "does a girl have to do for some company around here?"

That occasioned the right amount of lewd laughter before Jimmy shoved himself free of the others. He snatched the book from Lorelei's lap. "That was expensive," he snapped.

"You got a bargain," Lorelei observed.

"We'll see." He tucked it safely back into the guitar case as Bonzo brought her a bottle of beer.

"Thanks." Her smile lit her purple eyes.

Jimmy stepped between them. "Your name's Lorelei."

"That's right, James. Wanna get out of here?"

"You don't mess around, do you?"

She drained the beer and grinned. "Oh, yes, sir. I do mess around."

"Where's that wanker I saw you with earlier? At the magic shop?"

"Waiting in the car."

"Your boyfriend?"

"He wishes. He's just a driver. He works for my boss, too."

"What's your boss do?"

Lorelei stood up, switched her skirt back into place. "He's a star-maker."

She watched electricity race up Jimmy's spine. Oh, was it as simple as that? She was a little disappointed.

"What do you do for him?" Bobby asked, shoving his way into the conversation. He had his hand out.

Lorelei took it in hers. "I'm a talent scout."

"It's a shame you didn't see more of the show, then," Jimmy said.

"I liked what I saw. Maybe you'd all like to come to a party at my boss's place in Laurel Canyon?"

"When?"

"Now."

"Where's Peter?" Jimmy asked the others.

"Screw Peter," Lorelei suggested. "He's not your mom."

The fiend had doubled-parked the limo on Sunset Boulevard when Lorelei led the band out of the club. He opened the door and handed her inside. Lorelei accepted the assistance without a word.

The boys were respectful until the door closed them inside the car, then erupted into raucous laughter.

"I know," Lorelei agreed. "Isn't he hideous, poor thing?" She opened the minibar and pulled out a bottle of Jim Beam. "Anyone like a drink for the road?"

"What's your boss's name?" Jimmy asked.

"Nick Asmedai."

She put a glass of bourbon over ice in the silent bass player's hand, another in Bobby's, and a glass of neat bourbon in the drummer's. For Jimmy and herself, she added a touch of water. He wondered how she'd figured out their tastes so quickly. It had to be more than a good guess. Her eyes twinkled as she sipped her drink.

"What's he do, your boss? We already have an album, a tour set up. What can he do for us?"

"Everything else," Lorelei promised. "He can get you radio play. Bigger venues. Stadium shows. Pyrotechnics. A concert film. Are you traveling by bus this time? That's a rough life. You're going to be riding around much more than you're playing. America is *big*. Wouldn't flying be better? Maybe in your own private jet? You could play more shows in less time. That would give you more time to record the second album."

"Maybe he won't like us," the drummer threatened.

"Maybe you won't like him." Lorelei shrugged, which did interesting things to the front of her dress. "This is just a first date."

The car turned and began to climb.

Bobby leaned across Lorelei, to set his empty glass down in the minibar. He'd been uncharacteristically quiet. "Where'd you meet her, Jimmy?"

"We didn't meet," the guitarist answered. "I saw her in a jumble shop on Melrose this afternoon."

Lorelei leaned back so they could talk across her. Tension positively crackled in the car. She watched them like a cat.

"You invite her to the show tonight?"

"I didn't talk to her." Jimmy turned to Lorelei. "Was it coincidence, then, you there tonight?"

"Seeing you at *Les Livres Interdit* was coincidence. I'd heard the buzz about your show last night, so I was on my way to check out tonight's gig. It's my job."

Breaking his silence, the bass player observed, "You don't much look like an office girl."

"I don't much work in an office."

The car glided to a stop. The boys exchanged glances, then downed their drinks, as the driver opened the door. The drummer picked up the bottle of bourbon as he climbed out of the car.

The house, tucked in amongst the trees, wasn't impressive from the curb. There were enough lights on to show it was big, but suburban big, not mansion big. Lorelei led the way up the brick path and opened the door.

A roar of voices spilled out into the darkness. It wasn't late yet, but the party had been going on for hours.

The house seemed lit solely by candles. Gangs of them clustered in every corner and lined the windowsills. In the shadows between, the air swirled with marijuana smoke. The boys knotted together just inside the entryway, clocking the famous faces. Zappa was there, of course, with a coterie of freaks. One of those Monkees talked with Stephen Stills. And Morrison, encompassed by girls. Everywhere lounged pairs and trios of supernaturally pretty girls.

Lorelei said, "Make yourselves at home. There's beer in the fridge and someone's probably tending bar in the kitchen, if you'd like something harder. I'll go let the boss know you're here."

As soon as she passed out of earshot, Bobby leaned against Jimmy's shoulder to whisper, "I don't like the way her boss has no name."

"She said he was called Nick."

"That's not what she calls him."

Jimmy nodded. Lorelei was definitely more deferential than he planned to be. In the meantime, though, he could use something to drink—and something to eat, if there was food. He hadn't had time to grab a bite before Peter hustled them off to the show. Since he was here, he might as well enjoy the party.

Lorelei found him wolfing down a lamb kebab. She pressed up against him to say, "Floria gave me some windowpane. Want one?"

"I don't like hard drugs," Jimmy protested. "We got another show tomorrow…"

"Let tomorrow take care of itself," Lorelei purred. She popped a tiny square of gelatin under her tongue. "Haven't you always felt there was more to life than what you could see?"

"Yes," Jimmy hissed.

"This will help you see it."

He snatched the acid out of her hand, tossed it into his mouth, and washed it down with yet another glass of bourbon.

Lorelei led him out to the fresher air on the patio. She backed up against one of the Grecian columns decorating the terrace, caught Jimmy's hand and pulled him closer, caressing his fingers. "I've always had a thing for guitarist's hands," she said. Then she kissed him.

Jimmy took a half-step back, but Lorelei caught his head with one hand, pulled him back to meet her mouth. At the press of her lips against his, the music woke in his blood again.

Jimmy saw a flash of Lorelei dancing, alone in the crowd at the Whisky, purple slip straining across every curve.

As if she could hear the music, she shifted her hips against his, swaying in time to the pulse of his blood.

"This dress just barely stays on," Lorelei whispered in his ear.

"There are too many people," Jimmy protested.

"No one's watching us," Lorelei promised, but she led him around to the other side of the column. Beyond the trees edging the patio, the lights of LA twinkled in the distance.

He discovered her back was bare beneath her hair. Her skin felt so lush and warm. He traced the edges of the dress against her back, let his hands roam a little lower.

Lorelei shimmied enough to hike up her skirt against the

column. She had nothing on beneath it.

"Show me what those guitar-playing fingers can do," she invited.

God, she was wet. Jimmy found a rhythm she liked and she leaned back against the column, giving him room to play.

Jimmy sped up, watched her eyes roll closed. He couldn't believe his luck, having such a beautiful girl in his power. He varied his touch to make her quiver, then settled into a new rhythm.

Her body hummed and sang in his hand. He played her as if she were an instrument. He teased her, leading her up to the edge of orgasm, then danced backward. He kept his fingers on the outside of her, even though her shudders yearned for more.

He'd never seen a woman so comfortable with her own body. She wasn't putting on a show for him, or gauging his reactions, or anything more than taking pleasure in his touch. She enjoyed each caress like it was the perfect gift she'd just been waiting to unwrap.

Watching the pulse throb in her throat, he licked his lips. She smiled at the sound. She looked so serene, he pressed a little harder, maybe to the fringes of pain. She caught her lower lip in her teeth, but didn't protest. A tremor chased across her brow. The breath stopped in her throat.

"You want it?"

"Oh, yes, please."

So he made her come. Then he slowed down a notch, long enough that she could catch her breath, and pushed her into another orgasm. And another after that.

"I'm gonna fall over if you do that again," she confessed.

He laughed at her. She captured his wrist, pulled his hand up, covered in her juices. "Look at what you did to me," she marveled. Then she proceeded to lick his fingers clean.

When at last she'd tormented him enough, she glided over to the low stone wall that ringed the patio. She hopped up onto it and stretched out, still wearing those ridiculously high heels.

"I'm parched," she sighed.

"I am, too." He turned back to the party to raid the bar.

It looked like the end of days in the house. Two redheads had backed Bobby into an armchair: sisters, if not twins. One knelt between his knees while the other kissed him with an ardor even more unsettling than the blowjob. Jimmy turned away, only to find something more depraved going on everywhere his eye landed.

He grabbed an unattended bottle of vodka and fled back to the patio, where Lorelei remained, looking out over the lights of LA. She had transformed into a creature of flame and shadow, skin gone crimson beneath a dress of writhing smoke. Black membranous wings lay folded across her back like a cloak. Short spikes of horn rose on either side of her forehead, peeking from her luxuriant hair.

She smiled at him, but didn't make any other threatening moves. "The acid's kicked in, hasn't it?"

"What are you?" Jimmy gasped.

"You've known since you saw me at Daniel's."

"This is too much," he protested, clutching his head.

He didn't know where he was, how to get back to the Chateau in the valley below. Even if he dared brave the party again to find a phone, he had no idea where to tell a cab to come. He could go looking for the monster who'd brought them here in the limo, but he feared what his new eyes would show him.

"Don't, Jimmy. Just breathe." She got up slowly, reached a long-fingered hand to him. "Don't let fear make you do something stupid. You have an opportunity few people even recognize. Don't run away from the thing you want most. That's what *normal people* do." She said the last with an icy contempt that elevated him far above normal.

He took her hand, let her draw him to the edge of the patio. It was cantilevered out over the edge of the mountain, nothing below but darkness. Lorelei's grip on him was reassuringly strong.

Trembling, he sat with his back to the cliff. "What do you want?"

"To pay you back for that delicious foreplay with the best lay of your life."

"What else?"

She smiled carefully, but he glimpsed her sharpened teeth.

"What else would you like?"

"Why me?"

"You have talent, Jimmy. That's not always rewarded in this world."

He knew that to be true. A cold ball of resolve grounded him. "I want us to be the biggest band in the world."

"My boss will be glad to draw up the paperwork." Lorelei's long nails traced a shivery pattern on Jimmy's thigh. Pleased by his response, she slithered over him, easing him gently back on the parapet.

"We'll fall," he protested.

"I have wings."

She preempted his response with a kiss, sliding her wicked tongue into his mouth as her hands mastered his belt buckle and fly. She didn't bother to peel his jeans down. If he'd thought she was hot and wet before, now she was molten. She slid her wetness along the length of his shaft, then pulled far enough away that both of them knew he'd strained after her.

"You want it?" she whispered.

"Yes."

She took him slowly, drawing the penetration out so that he went half mad with craving. By the time he was deep inside her, it felt like home.

"Open your eyes," she suggested.

Heat rose from her skin in wisps that coiled upward, spelling out runes. The dress swirled around her like smoke, knitting rosettes and lace, always on the move. Lorelei's hips took up a slow, bluesy rhythm that woke the music in Jimmy's blood. He knew she could hear it, but was she dancing to it or did she create it?

"It's all you, sorcerer," she whispered. "You call the tune and I'll dance."

So he fucked her as hard and deep as he could. He dug his fingers into her haunches, but she didn't fight him or pull away. She only laughed, delighted, and rode him, while the music crashed and wailed in his head, and the magic flowed all around him.

When it was over, finally over, Jimmy felt like he'd never felt before. Simultaneously drained and exhilarated, his body felt as if it could topple over into sleep, while his brain burned, on fire.

Lorelei lit a pair of cigarettes with the tip of one nail: not magic so much as a function of what she was. She handed one cigarette to him and smoked the other contemplatively. He wondered what she was thinking.

The house behind them shimmered with magic. Signs and sigils marked its stones, scrawled across its doorway. Jimmy couldn't begin to read what it said. He barely recognized a mark here and there. The promise of so much hidden knowledge pierced him. What would he be able to do if he understood all of that?

Lorelei crushed her cigarette out on the stone parapet beside her leg. "Would you like to meet my master?"

"Master?" Jimmy echoed.

"You know the truth now. Have you guessed who he is?"

"The Prince of this World?"

She laughed, but didn't deny it. "Asmodeus, Prince of Lechers."

She caught his hand and pulled him forward a few steps, before noticing he wanted a moment to reassemble his clothing. "You needn't worry," she promised. "He's seen worse."

Inside the house, the party had wound down. People sprawled, passed out on every piece of furniture. More of them were human than Jimmy expected, but he watched another devil girl close the refrigerator door, a bottle of champagne in her hand. Where Lorelei was curvy and dark, this willowy succubus was blond as a ray of light.

"He's ready for you," the blonde said. "I'll bring the glasses."

Lorelei led Jimmy down a winding stair. The cavern under the house had probably started as a wine cellar, but now served as a throne room. On a gilded chair sat a beautiful dark man with hair coiled like lamb's wool. He'd draped one leg over the chair's arm and toyed with a walking stick. As Jimmy stepped forward, heart hammering in his ears, his perception of the demon flickered between the man and a huge angelic creature with a leg so twisted it would be a miracle if he could walk.

"So you want your band to be number one in the world," Asmodeus said. His voice rang with dark harmonies. "What do you offer in exchange?"

"My soul."

"Will you sign the contract here before you?" Asmodeus gestured with his stick. Lorelei took Jimmy's elbow, nudged him over to the rostrum.

"Read it first," Lorelei advised, but Jimmy couldn't focus his eyes. The words coiled and crawled around each other, layers deep. When he looked up, she offered him an antique knife, ruby-crusted handle first.

Jimmy saw a flash of himself thrusting the blade into Lorelei's heart, then racing up the stairs away from here. The image made him laugh. Without hesitation, he drew the knife shallowly across the meat of his forearm, where it would draw blood but not impact his guitar playing. Lorelei set the knife aside, dipped Jimmy's fingers in his blood, and pressed them to the foot of the contract.

"Champagne?" the other succubus asked.

Lorelei helped Jimmy round up Jonesy, Bonzo, and Bobby, and get them into the car. She was disappointed that Jimmy had flinched when he could have asked for what he wanted more than fame: power. He might have become the world's most dangerous sorcerer, but he'd chosen music over magic. She wondered if he'd ever be self-aware enough to regret it. By then, he'd have nothing of value left to trade in.

The sun crept over the horizon as the car rolled back up the drive to the Chateau Marmont.

"Coming up?" Jimmy asked as the others shambled back into the hotel toward bed.

"I'm not part of your contract," Lorelei pointed out.

"Be my girl in LA?" He wriggled his fingers and held out his hand.

Lorelei grinned as she took it.

Grandfather Carp's Dream

Long after midnight at a university in the north, a graduate student hunched over the plants he was grafting. In the silence, a woman's voice sang something lovely. The graduate student's head jerked up. The woman continued to sing, her voice as melancholy as the winter winds outside the botanical research facility. The graduate student wished he could understand her words. They reminded him of the Japanese he'd heard spoken behind the counter of his favorite sushi restaurant.

He shook himself. No one was supposed to be in the garden at this hour.

Quietly, he crept to the glass door that connected the research wing to the botanical garden. At the edge of the Temperate House pool, a woman sat gazing into the water. As she sang to the carp floating in the pool, she ran a white comb through her black, black hair, hair so long it swayed almost to the floor.

The graduate student opened the door into the garden. When the woman glanced up, her eyes flared golden. The graduate student wished he could speak Japanese so he could ask why she was so sad. Instead, in English, he demanded, "What are you doing here?"

In English, she replied, "I am a dream of Grandfather Carp."

Before the graduate student could puzzle that out, the heavy door slipped from his hand. It clanged shut. When he turned back toward the pool, the woman had disappeared.

He hadn't heard the sound of running, so she couldn't have gone far. Unfortunately, the garden received light only through the glass roof and the research wing door. She had a variety of shadows in which to hide.

"Come out." His voice echoed the sadness of her song as he walked down the stone steps to the pond.

The light trickling in from the research wing spilled pale and golden across the small pond. The largest carp rose to the water's surface to gulp air. Should the graduate student have measured, the fish was as long as his forearm from fingertip to elbow. Occasionally, garden visitors joked that the single fish would feed a family. Now the carp seemed to be the one laughing.

With a sigh, the graduate student returned to the research wing to call university security. He hoped they would find the intruder before she damaged the plants.

Next afternoon, when the student returned to the botanical research facility, his mind was too full of notes for his dissertation to recall last night's mysterious visitor. So he was surprised to see the woman perched on the side of the pool when he entered the garden. She dipped a hand between the lilies and cupped up some water. A sparrow swooped down from the ficus tree to drink from her palm.

Sometimes birds slipped in through the ventilation grills, he told himself. Although it was winter and unlikely, the grills might have been open a crack. This can't be as weird as it seems, he assured himself.

"You must help me." Even her accent was musical and melancholy.

He joined her on the pool's ledge. She wore a kimono of shimmering aquamarine over a spectrum of blue and green undergarments. Her ebony hair piled onto her head, held by a mother-of-pearl comb. Her upturned face seemed made of porcelain. When she smiled, a wish formed in his heart. "I'll be glad to help, if you don't run away," he promised.

"Grandfather Carp desires to be free. He conjured me to persuade you to release him from the lily pond."

The graduate student stared at her, disappointed that she was crazy.

"Believe your heart," she urged, touching a delicate finger to his chest.

Delicious warmth tingled throughout his body. Yes, he had been lonely and, yes, she *was* beautiful. Sheepishly, he began to formulate a plan.

He waited in his beat-up old Buick in the parking lot until

everyone left the facility for the night. He wanted no one to see what he planned to do. Equipment in hand, he trudged through the gray slush of February and into the glass dome of the garden.

The falling water in the Temperate House sounded like chimes. It trickled down the mossy rock wall, rolled off the ferns, dripped staccato allegro into the pool. Above the water skimmed iridescent dragonflies. Blue, green, purple: they performed a complex geometric dance.

A bright shadow, the color of the first morning sunlight, rose through the murky water. It skulked beneath a round Nymphea Baghdad leaf, then flashed up to eat the loveliest dragonfly.

Shocked, the student stared at the rings left on the water by the carp's passage. He had a fantasy that the naiad lay beneath the surface of the pool, gazing sweetly at him from beneath the lily leaves. The biggest carp swam between the two of them, rolling its black eyes. Self-satisfaction lurked in its wide-mouthed grin.

After filling the bucket, the graduate student picked up the long-handled pool skimmer. It had the sturdiest net he could find this time of year.

The carp leered as it leapt into the net.

The bucket grew heavier as the graduate student lugged it up the bowed concrete steps to his apartment. When he paused to unlock his door, the fish thrashed threateningly.

In the corner of the student's living room, the filter of his new fish tank chugged merrily. Before the student could reach it, the carp threw itself to the floor. The student dropped to his knees and grabbed the fish's tail, but it wriggled out of reach. He crawled after it.

"What are you doing? Grandfather wanted to be freed into a river."

Startled by the nymph's sudden appearance, the student stumbled over the bucket, spilling the last of the water into his ragged brown carpeting. He gestured awkwardly at his tiny breakfast nook, set with flowers, candles, his best unchipped plates. "I wanted to invite you to dinner. I didn't think you'd come if the fish wasn't invited, too."

Her golden eyes narrowed. "What's on the menu?"

"Tofu stir-fry for us. Mealworms for the fish."

Blushing sweetly, the naiad joined them on the floor. "Let me help you catch him."

Within seconds, she cradled the carp in her arms, a Japanese Madonna—only not quite so serene. Damp splotched her kimono. Her hair spilled out of its careful arrangement. She released the carp into the huge fish tank, where it swam furiously back and forth.

In the awkward silence, the student asked, "What's your name?"

"Jiyo."

"Jiyo. That's pretty. What's it mean?"

"Liberty." Jiyo turned from the fish tank to look at the student. "Jack," she said, and he wondered how she knew his name, "Grandfather is very unhappy in this tank. But he consents to me having dinner with you, if you will then let him go afterward."

"I can't." To forestall her protests, he raised his hands—palm out—and added, "Didn't the fish notice how cold it was outside? The river is frozen over until spring. Even if I could chip through the ice and release him, he'd freeze to death. I will return him to the Temperate House pool after we eat. I swear I'll release him in the spring. But this trip tonight was purely selfish on my part. I'm sorry."

Jiyo faced the tank again. Jack got the feeling she was translating for the carp. He left them alone while he put on some dry clothes.

When he returned, Jiyo was combing her long silken hair, humming quietly to herself. Her robes seemed to have dried already. A single blue dragonfly darted over the fish tank.

"Grandfather will stay here until spring," Jiyo announced. "Fewer fish to share the tank with."

"Great!" Jack said, then less enthusiastically, "He *will* eat whatever wildlife he imports in here, won't he?"

Jiyo shrugged and started to put up her hair. "Why don't you make dinner?"

Affamé

His stomach growled mournfully. Sean Liu wondered if those dumpstered egg rolls were formulating a plan of attack or simply wishing for company. Damn, he missed his mom's cooking.

"Got a light?"

Sean stopped scanning passing cars to acknowledge the boy who'd walked up. He was taller than Sean, dark and slim in his Oakland Raiders jacket. Sean pulled a book of matches—from the club down the block—out of his jeans. What did the older boy want? Sean was working, standing outside the shuttered bookstore on Polk Street, hoping for a place to spend the night.

This part of San Francisco was a transitional zone between the squalor of the Tenderloin and the bright residences of Nob Hill. Further down the street clustered the bars of Polk Gulch, where the older men who'd fled the disco throb of the Castro came to drink and fight. Sean couldn't pass for 21, which increased his value on the street, but made it impossible to work inside a bar where he might feel warm and safe.

The boy in the Raiders jacket held out a pack of Marlboros. Out of courtesy, Sean took one. The last thing he wanted was to set anyone off, get himself bashed, and have to squat someplace until the bruises healed.

"I'm Kasim," the older boy said, setting a cigarette between his lips and striking a match. Sean leaned close to take the light. Kasim continued, "It's cold to be working this late."

So Kasim recognized what Sean was doing in the fringes of the Tenderloin after midnight. Maybe Kasim had done it, too.

"I'm hoping things pick up after bar closing," Sean said.

"Need a place to stay?"

Sean couldn't figure the kid out. He seemed relaxed, like chatting up working boys was something he often did. But he didn't seem to be picking up on Sean, either. The lack of vibes was creepy. He was out of place on Polk at this hour: too young for the bars, expensive Nikes on his feet, hair neatly faded, diamonds in both ears. Not living on the street, at any rate. Maybe his Daddy put him up somewhere warm.

"Someplace to stay would be good," Sean agreed.

Kasim blew out a long plume of smoke. "Let's walk over to Van Ness and catch a cab."

Full of questions, Sean trailed the older boy over a block. He didn't get any heat off Kasim at all. He seemed like a messenger, sent to pick up new meat to sate someone else's appetite. Sean wondered if Kasim had been looking specifically for Chinese boys.

The wind gusted hard and cold off San Francisco Bay, running down the length of Van Ness. Sean shivered. He suspected he ought to make nice, in case he needed an ally later. Although Kasim appeared to be running the errand willingly, he might turn mean once Sean got between him and his meal ticket.

A Fog City Cab pulled up and Kasim climbed in. With a grin, he asked, "Coming?"

Grinning back, Sean wondered what his skin tasted like.

The cab dropped them off in a desolate stretch of industrial buildings, not far from the afterhours EndUp Club, but miles away from the Victorian row houses of the Castro or the quiet streets of Potrero Hill. Nothing moved on this street. A scream here would blow away between the warehouses and vanish into the fog.

Kasim paid the cabdriver, then led Sean down an unlighted alley. In the distance, a bare bulb burned above a nondescript metal door.

Sean worded and reworded his question. The best he could come up with was, "Have you stayed here long?"

From the shadows, Kasim answered, "Almost six months."

"You get treated well?"

"Better 'n anywhere else."

Once the darkness engulfed them both, the older boy rounded on Sean and pushed him back against a cinderblock wall. "Are you a cocksucker, Sean?"

The kid had played it *so* cool. Sean reached for Kasim's waistband and deftly undid the fly. Kasim's dick was hard in Sean's hand. Sean slid to his knees, eyes closed against the darkness around them. Kissing or cocksucking: he could never do either with his eyes open.

Kasim tasted salty and sweet, his sweat clean after a recent shower. Sean knew his own body wasn't nearly as fresh. The questions hadn't left his brain, but he pushed them aside, concentrating instead on gliding slowly up and down the length of Kasim's shaft, letting the older boy enjoy the difference between Sean's hot mouth and spit gone cold in the dark alley.

Unexpectedly, Kasim wrenched away. Cum struck Sean's cheek and leather jacket, ropy and almost phosphorescent in the dim light.

Before Sean could speak, a huge force swept him off the alley floor and thrust him hard against the wall. As he struggled to recapture his breath, a single hand pinned him like an insect, feet dangling in mid-air.

Someone licked him from collarbone to temple, lapping up Kasim's still-warm cum. The tongue itself could hardly be human, it was so icy and rough. Sean wriggled, trying to see what held him in place.

Its accent softly French, a deep voice rumbled, "Does he give good head?"

"Yeah." Kasim zipped himself back up. "It was hard to stop him in time."

"Hard to decide you wanted him to stop," the Frenchman corrected.

"Yeah," Kasim admitted. "His name is Sean."

"Well, Sean," the Frenchman purred, "if you join us here, you'll have to do more than suck cock."

Sean's own dick twitched in response to that. If Kasim had let him go on much longer, he would have had it out and gotten himself some relief. Now he was stranded between arousal and fear. He managed to say, "Yes, sir."

The man—it had to be a man—leaned closed to Sean, rubbing a bearded cheek against Sean's clean-shaven face. "You have to take me up your ass, Sean."

His free hand explored Sean's fly, stroking Sean's dick through the denim with an insistent strength that melted the last of the boy's uncertainty and made his fear much more piquant.

"Yes, sir. I can do that."

"Good."

The pressure on his chest eased. Sean's feet touched the alley floor.

"Clean him up, Kasim. Make it quick. I'm hungry."

Kasim opened the door beneath the bare bulb to reveal an unlit warehouse full of hulking equipment and the smell of dust. "You can use my shower," Kasim offered. "Up here."

Sean turned back to watch the shadow-man's entrance, but the door closed without revealing him.

"He'll want you soon," Kasim said. "We better get you cleaned up first."

Following the older boy up the industrial-grade metal stairs, Sean wondered, "Does he have a name?"

"It's Guillaume. But you're smarter to keep calling him 'sir.' He's hella old-fashioned."

That pronouncement came without a trace of irony. Sean understood that respect flowed outward. He was used to that from home, with the uncles and aunties he had been expected to revere, whether they deserved it or not. He could certainly play the game. Eighteen years of growing up a first-generation American had prepared him for it. He hoped it didn't mean suffering an unrequited boner all goddamn night.

The stairs led to a small suite of loft rooms. Kasim's unmade bed dominated the first, its black comforter spilled onto the floor. Bose speakers, a flat-screen TV, and PlayStation completed the décor. Everything looked shiny.

"Shower's through there." Kasim waved at one of the doors. "I'll bring you a towel."

That sounded promising. Sean went into the bathroom, closed the door to piss, then opened it a crack before he turned the shower on.

The fixtures were all new, if nothing expensive. Sean

wondered if the loft was a recent addition, space for Kasim so he wouldn't be continuously under Guillaume's feet.

Sean stepped out of his tennis shoes. They'd been expensive, bought by his mom before his senior year of high school. Right before he'd been busted for hustling the first time. After the court-mandated counseling hadn't managed to turn him straight—not that it had ever promised to, despite his pop's fondest wishes—Sean had been thrown out of the house. The Supreme Court might sanction gay sex, but Pop still ruled his own little world. He couldn't face the shame of having a gay son, so he erased Sean, disowned him, preferring to speak of him as dead than explain to his colleagues why Sean wouldn't date their wannabe immigrant nieces.

Sean had already sold the other treasures he'd walked away with: the Rolex (his coming-of-age gift from Pop), the North Beach Leather jacket, the iPod. Sean would've taken his Mitsubishi too, but undoubtedly Pop would've turned him in as a car thief. The loss of a son was easier to countenance than the loss of a car.

The clothes Sean stripped out of had come out of a box at Glide Memorial Church, where Sean sometimes ate meals. He left everything in a mound, then stepped into the shower stall.

Before long Kasim joined him. Sean traced his fingers across the other boy's chest, admiring the brown of his skin, tight spirals of black fur across his breastbone, heavy steel rings gleaming in his nipples. Kasim grinned as he shoved Sean's hands away. "This is business," he said. "Got to make sure you sparkle."

Kasim grabbed the bar of soap and lathered Sean's dick, which grew harder by the second.

"Don't let me get you too worked up," Kasim growled playfully, reaching for more soap. He sudsed Sean's balls thoroughly, working his fingers over the skin to an almost clinical degree. Sean wondered at the inspection. Kasim hadn't shown any hesitation about the hygiene of Sean's mouth.

Kasim play-slapped Sean's hip. "Turn around and wash that off, but don't fool with yourself. Guillaume will want to drink your first load."

Sean whispered, "You won't tell, will you?"

Kasim nipped Sean's shoulder. Sean turned into the kiss and their tongues met. Sean leaned back against the cool tile to enjoy the length of Kasim's slick body against his own. Kasim caught Sean's hands and forced them back against the wall. He ground his dick against Sean's hip, then broke the kiss. "It's not worth getting caned for you, baby, so yeah: I'd tell him in a New York minute if you come without permission."

Sean swallowed hard. "Does he really cane you?"

"When I deserve it."

Sean's erection faded. "If I get so worked up that I can't help myself..."

"He'd cane me 'cuz you're new and don't know the house rules. Which is why I'm trying to school you, baby. I won't tell you there's nothing to be afraid of," he said, pushing Sean into the shower spray, "'cuz Guillaume can be a scary motherfucker, without even trying. I think being scared can be really hot. Guillaume is the hottest thing I ever met."

"How long has he been your boyfriend?"

Kasim laughed, flashing blue-white teeth. "He's not my boyfriend. He's my dom."

Sean wondered what kind of dominant drank cum. Who in his right mind submitted to being caned for cumming without permission?

Kasim apparently felt that he'd scared Sean enough. "Look, you can walk out of here now, if you want. I'll give you the fare and call you a cab. You can wait for it at the bus stop on the corner. But if you leave, you'll be walking away from the hottest sex of your life."

"And he'll beat you, won't he?"

"Yeah. And then he'll fuck me."

"How can that be okay?" Sean demanded.

"Stick around. You won't be sorry," Kasim promised. "Really, Sean: walking away from Guillaume is a mistake you'll regret. For the rest of your life, you'll be dreaming about what you missed."

"But I'll *have* a rest of my life."

"Sean, man, you live on the fucking street. What kind of life is that?"

That rocked Sean. For the briefest second, he'd forgotten that he wasn't going home to the mansion in Seacliff, that he wasn't attending Stanford in the fall, that he wasn't headed for a glorious future in his pop's office at the Bank of Hong Kong. He was sleeping in doorways and showering at the Y and turning tricks on Polk Street.

"Perspective, man, that's all I'm saying. Get the sex first, I'll buy you breakfast, then you can split if you want to."

"I don't want to be beaten to death and chopped up and thrown into the Bay."

"The cab driver saw where we went. He'll have the address in his log. Guillaume would be pretty fucking stupid to leave a trail like that."

Not that anyone would report him missing, Sean realized. If he stopped showing up on Polk, the guys he hung out with would assume he'd found a Daddy and settled down, or gone back to his parents, or moved to LA or Portland to check out different trade. Unless his body washed up on the beach, he'd just vanish.

Kasim smoothed back Sean's wet hair. "Don't worry about it, little brother. I'm not gonna let anything happen to you that you don't beg for first. I promise. The thing I love most about Guillaume, the reason I trust him with my life, is that he never does anything without getting permission first. He won't beat you unless you're asking for it. He won't kill you unless you convince him that there's nothing you want more in all the world. And I'm telling you that once he fucks you, that's all you're ever gonna want again. So turn around. Let's get that skanky street ho ass of yours scrubbed clean enough to eat from and get you down to business."

They swathed themselves in black bath sheets that wrapped around Sean four times. He contemplated the heap of his dirty clothes and wished he had anything clean to wear.

The lights went off. "He's ready," Kasim explained. "Are you?"

As stiff as when he'd sucked Kasim's dick in the alley, Sean said, "Yeah."

"Hand over the towel."

Sean did. Kasim enfolded him in something that felt like sheepskin, long soft fur that caressed his bare skin. It hung over his face, but he felt swaddled rather than suffocated. "That's to keep you from getting chilled," Kasim explained.

Sean was swept up in someone's arms and bent across a strong shoulder. His arms and legs were free in case he felt like struggling. Nothing blocked his mouth. More amused than frightened, he kept still.

They left Kasim's rooms. Boots clomped down the metal stairs. Sean was pretty sure the person carrying him was Guillaume: the strength seemed so certain of itself. He didn't know if Kasim could lift him, let alone carry him down steps.

They crossed the cement floor of the warehouse. After a slight pause while a door opened, Sean was laid across a firm mattress. The air smelled enclosed—Sean couldn't have said why—and was warmed by a crackling fire.

Sean's stomach grumbled.

He heard a soft chuckle. "Are you hungry, beautiful boy? Kasim, go order some hamburgers."

Sean heard the door close again. He was alone with Guillaume. A shiver ran through him.

He was carefully unwrapped. Guillaume knelt above him. Brown hair fell to the Frenchman's shoulders in soft waves. Dark eyes glittered avidly in the firelight, exploring Sean's body. Guillaume's short beard covered the lower half of his face with dense fur. He looked like a carefully styled Eurotrash model, Sean would have said, except that the harness he wore above his leather jeans wrapped him so deliciously—emphasizing pecs and shoulders and rippled stomach—that Sean didn't feel judgmental.

Guillaume unsnapped a strap around his wrist. He lifted Sean's balls and wrapped the leather beneath them, snugging them close to the shaft of his cock. The band wasn't uncomfortable, but definitely focused Sean's attention in a new way.

"Okay?"

Sean nodded, not trusting his voice. He was afraid to sound like an eager, frightened kid.

"Roll over."

Sean turned over on the sheepskin.

Guillaume's strong fingers massaged his back, working into the knot of muscle above his tailbone. Sean's fears that the older man was measuring him for stripes amped up when Guillaume issued his next command: "Hands and knees. I don't want you grinding your hips into the mattress."

Sean did as told, wondering if there would be any negotiation tonight.

The Frenchman traced his fingers between Sean's buttocks, teasing the boy into wriggling backward. Sean gasped when the anticipated fingers were replaced by a rough, cold, very wet tongue.

The sensation was unlike any Sean had ever felt. Rather than the insistent probe of solid fingers, he felt like a kitten being lapped clean by its mother: more intimate and embarrassing than the scrubbing Kasim had given him upstairs. Sean pressed his burning face against the cool white cotton sheet, but didn't squirm away from Guillaume's exploring tongue. Instead, he pushed himself backward, trying to internalize more of it, to peel himself open and expose more nerves.

The sensations, Sean realized, were slowly driving him mad. The physiological limitations of tongue and anus couldn't provide the stimulation he craved. He wanted to feel something deep inside him. He wanted to be filled, worn like a piece of clothing, possessed.

The etiquette of the situation escaped him. This was the last place he expected to be: ass in the air, dancing on the tip of the master's tongue. Kasim's talk of beatings made Sean hesitant to ask for anything not readily offered.

His dick throbbed where it hung in mid-air. As soon as Sean thought about the cock ring, Guillaume's fingers stroked the swollen sac of his balls. Sean moaned.

"You have to say?"

"Please, sir. You said you would fuck me."

"How much do you want it?"

Low in his throat, Sean said truthfully, "I want it more than anything."

Guillaume traced a feather touch up the underside of Sean's

dick. Sean groaned.

"More than cumming yourself?"

"I'll change my mind if you do that a few more times," Sean growled. "'Til then, I want to feel your dick inside me. Please."

Sean listened intently as Guillaume unzipped his leather jeans and slipped out of them. Then the master's cock slid up between Sean's buttocks, teasing him.

"Oh, God," Sean breathed, shivering.

Guillaume laughed. "You want it, pretty boy? Show me how hungry you are."

Sean wasn't sure what that meant. Most tricks wanted to stuff themselves inside him, hump like feral weasels, then hurry home to their wives with some lie about how hard it is to find a decent chardonnay. Indecision froze the boy in place, but the hard dick just outside his reach raised tears in his eyes.

Guillaume pressed forward the slightest bit. "Come on, Sean. Aren't you hungry?"

Sean expelled the frustrated breath he'd been holding and pushed backward. Guillaume held his dick in place, letting the boy impale himself.

This also was like nothing he'd ever felt before. The sense of control was heady. Sean forced himself not to rush anything, using the pressure and release of his body around Guillaume's shaft to inflame the older man, trying to tantalize him into losing control and slamming his dick home.

Guillaume apparently had other ideas. He wrapped one arm around Sean's waist, the other across his shoulders. "When you're done playing with me, why don't you sit up?"

With a slight shift of his balance, he pulled the boy backward onto his lap. Sean found himself sitting atop Guillaume's absurdly muscular thighs.

"That's it." Guillaume nipped Sean's neck. "Now show me how good you can fuck me."

Trembling, Sean experimented with pistoning himself up and down. Sweat trickled down his chest.

"Open your eyes," Guillaume ordered. "See how beautiful you look, fucking me?"

Sean realized that the wall beside the bed was mirrored. He

had to fight not to cum at the mere sight.

Something moved behind him. His eyes focused on a figure over his shoulder in the mirror: Kasim, wreathed in shadows. He wore a harness like Guillaume's, his dick pointing like a broomstick from the silver ring at his crotch.

Catching Sean's eye, Kasim stroked his shaft once.

Quivering, Sean locked his muscles up, fighting the twitch in his cock, desperate not to cum.

"Get over here and catch it," Guillaume commanded. "And you'd better not miss a fucking drop."

Kasim captured Sean's dick with his mouth. His lips had barely closed when Sean lost it. He dug his fingers into Kasim's nape, thrusting wildly as he came.

Kasim caught it all. As Sean settled down, the other boy crawled up onto the bed to sandwich Sean between his body and Guillaume's. He leaned forward to kiss his master, feeding him tonguefuls of Sean's cum.

Sean shuddered as the two men continued to pass his cum between them. Swallowing cum was one thing. Feeding it to someone else was quite another. He hoped he'd never be called on to do it.

And with that thought, Sean realized that he hoped he would be invited to join this twisted ménage. One night wasn't enough to explore how low the others would go. Sean grinned at his reflection in the mirror.

As Guillaume swallowed the secondhand cum, he lost his own control, pounding his dick up into Sean, thrashing and cumming and growling deep in his throat like a beast. Sean clung to Kasim just to stay upright.

Without warning, Guillaume pushed Sean aside. He lunged forward onto Kasim, knocking him sprawling. The boy's legs looked bent at a painful angle, held in place by Guillaume's weight.

The Frenchman swallowed Kasim's dick in a gulp. He gnawed it with his teeth, driving Kasim into a squirming, whimpering frenzy. Sean couldn't imagine how much the bites must hurt, but Kasim didn't especially seem to mind.

Sean felt extraneous. After that incredible fuck, the

disappointment of being cast off stung. He felt like he had when wandering the streets of Chinatown after his pop kicked him out, like a broken little boy who wanted to cry. He curled up on the edge of the bed, hugging himself.

Kasim begged incoherently for permission to cum. He twisted the ring in his left nipple like it was some kind of key. Guillaume reached up, slapped Kasim's hand away, and yanked hard on the ring, stretching the skin away from the boy's chest.

As if that was the signal he'd been waiting for, Kasim came, shouting and convulsing and praising God and Guillaume.

And Guillaume's head didn't stop bobbing until he'd slurped every drop of cum from Kasim's dick.

The boy looked totally spent as Guillaume sat up and rubbed his beard dry with one hand. "Thank you, boys. You can go now. Your dinner will probably be ready."

Weak-kneed, Kasim pushed himself off the bed. He waved for Sean to help him walk. In the flickering firelight, his dick looked bruised already.

Sean waited until the bedroom door was closed behind him to ask, "What was that?"

Kasim grinned. "Guillaume was famished." He handed Sean a plush black robe and began to pull on his clothes. "I'm gonna run out and pick up our burgers."

Sean followed him back to the industrial stairs and asked, "What do you mean: he was famished?"

"He lives on cum. It's all he eats. Well, and blood. But he prefers cum. How did it feel to be on the menu?"

"You're joking, right?"

"Baby, I don't joke about Guillaume. He's got some complicated tastes, telling me what to eat to vary the flavor for him. But every now and again, he wants something different."

"And tonight he wanted Chinese takeout."

"C'mon, man, don't be like that. You're not hurt because he didn't want to snuggle afterward?" Kasim pulled Sean toward him and kissed him hard, lips mashed between teeth, hands full of Sean's ass. Sean twisted the nipple ring until Kasim's knees went weak.

"I'll give you all the snuggling you want, little brother,"

Kasim promised. "I've got a whole box full of toys I can't wait to share with you. We can get ourselves wound up until our balls turn blue…"

And Guillaume would swoop in to gulp down the results. Sean's dick jumped at the thought.

"Climb in bed and keep yourself warm," Kasim directed. "I'll be back in two shakes."

Mothflame

Stainless steel buildings reflected the traffic whirling around me as I walked in the street. The city hadn't bothered to rebuild the sidewalks after the big quake. Why would they? No one but me walked outside any longer. I clutched the crucifix under my jacket and prayed, *Let this be the end of my search.*

I followed familiar streets to the carport of Tony's apartment building. A camera catalogued my appearance before it allowed me to enter.

The lobby echoed with the sound of the rusty fountain. The elevator operator's face twitched into a smile when she recognized me. When I asked for Tony's penthouse, she took me up in silence.

His door was still coded to my hand. I'd dropped out, vanished, and of course Tony had forgotten to erase the computer. Some days Tony forgot where he lived.

When I pushed the door open, I heard him in the bedroom with someone loud and worshipful. At least he still had groupies. I sat on the scarred black leather sofa. As ever, the penthouse stank of bongwater and spoiled food. Moldy glasses littered every flat surface. Sweet God, I had called this place home for two years. Had I been so painfully young?

Before long, Tony wandered out of the bedroom to stick his head into the refrigerator. Then he spun to stare at me. "God damn. Chris?"

Out on the street, I might not have recognized him. His cheeks were so sunken that it looked as if he'd had his back teeth removed. He was still hooked, that much was certain.

"I need your help," I said. "I need to meet Ysanne."

"Jesus, Christy, where've you been?" Tony rounded the kitchen counter and advanced on me. "I can't believe you just walked back in here."

I stood, wishing that the coffee table hadn't pinned my legs so close to the sofa. Tony flung his arms out and hugged me, crushing me against his hollow ribs. "How've you been?" he demanded, leering. "You're looking great—not a kid anymore."

"Tony, do you know anything about Ysanne?" I pushed against his clammy chest and wished he had thrown on a robe.

He curled under questioning, as always. "She's doing a sold-out show at the Capitol tonight."

"Know anyone holding tickets?"

"No." He rubbed his arms. "She's alienated the business. But there's a club in the basement of the San Pedro where her people hang."

I flexed my shoulders inside my jacket; I was stiff with nerves. I had dreaded this meeting with Tony. Pathetic Tony, ex-sex rock god. "Thanks."

"Hey, you aren't leavin', are you?" He grabbed my arm. "I just got a crate in from Zululand..."

"I'm less interested than ever, Tony."

"At least, stay and talk. I haven't seen you in years! Where ya been? Who ya been doin'? You can't sneak in here, demand answers about some religious freak, and disappear again. What makes you think I'd let you pull that crap?"

His sharpened nails clawed across my leather sleeve as I pulled away. I navigated the scattered refuse to the door. "One more hit and you won't remember I was here, Tony. Just like the last time."

"You're not worth rememberin', Christy. Just a groupie!" he shrieked. "Slut!"

I walked away. This time he remembered to reset the computer. When I stepped onto the elevator, I heard glass shatter as his fist went through the screen.

Ysanne's album was playing when I opened the door to the packed basement club. I joined the cluster of young people at the bar. They stared at my coat, the battered leather worn tan. It had been years since there had been enough cows to produce leather. Drifting out of my way, the kids watched me order a synthbeer.

A girl with bleached hair and a large black pillbox hat leaned against the chrome bar. Her shoulder pressed against mine. "Buy me a drink?"

I laid a couple bills on the bar and signaled the bartender to come back. It rolled over, squeaking on elderly treads, and the girl ordered. Wheezing, the bartender spewed alcohol into a glass.

"Aren't you a little old for this kind of place?" The girl's voice was consciously breathy.

"I'm looking for a ticket to Ysanne's concert tonight."

Without another word, she picked up her glass and joined a nearby table.

One of the boys there smiled, watching me watch her. Not the cunning, appraising smiled that preluded a pick-up, but that would come with practice. He was a child. My insides shredded.

After listening to her with half his attention, he came over and stood too close. "Bindi says you don't have a ticket to see Ysanne tonight."

"I also don't have much in the way of money."

"Who does?"

"What would your extra ticket cost?"

"Nothing you couldn't part with." He toyed with a painted fan that hung on a red silk cord from his belt. "Come home?"

I left the untouched beer on the bar and followed him.

His room was papered in silver foil, reflective enough to throw back smudges of movement, but not faces, not details. As he paced, an army of ghosts paced with him. The sensation recalled everything I disliked about the city.

He called himself Aden. He said he was a model and showed me a chip collection of the commercials he'd done. While I watched it, he pulled a sealed plastic box from under the sofa and set it on the green glass table. Inside were syringes in sterile wrappings, a white porcelain crucible, a steel-tank lighter. Aden twisted open a pill capsule, spilling its azure and emerald fillings into the crucible.

I broke open the heavy plastic around a syringe and fitted in a needle. Aden looked pleased when I handed it to him.

"As a kid," I said, "I had to shoot heroin into my boyfriend when he was too messed up to do it himself. He said I gave painless shots."

The videochip muttered about men's colognes and shiny sports cars and flavors of Everclear. Aden sighed as the needle slipped under his skin. His face spasmed, ecstatic, orgasmic. I wondered if he enjoyed anything else as much.

His eyes, hazy green under black lashes, refocused on me. "Shall I mix yours light?"

"None for me, thanks." I slipped my boots off. "Could I use your shower?"

He directed me to the bath, which was tiled in reflective black. I turned the water on very hot. While my back was turned, Aden peeled into a full-body sheath. He wrestled me to the floor and fought the jeans off of me. He held his hand over my mouth as he climbed over my body. I took the hint. He wanted me to stay quiet. I closed my eyes and pretended he was Ysanne.

After he left me, I took a long hot shower. When I pushed the black curtain back, my reflection spilled out, rippling over the tiles. Aden had turned on the fan.

Back out in front of the videoscreen, he was wrapped in a canary yellow robe, watching a video of Ysanne. I pulled a purple T-shirt out of my backpack and over my head.

"I could lend you something to wear to the concert," Aden offered.

"This'll be fine." I stepped into my last pair of clean jeans.

When I had dressed, he suggested, "Come watch this."

I sat next to him, but he didn't touch me. I appreciated it. Aden said Ysanne had seen him in some awful porn flick. Her people had contacted him to appear in her video. It concerned a spaceman who had concluded, from watching television, that the most influential people in America were young blond women. So the spaceman built such a body and locked himself inside.

"Who did you play?" I asked as Aden restarted the recording.

"Ysanne as the alien. Before she came to earth."

He disappeared into the bathroom, leaving his drug paraphernalia out. I concentrated on the videoscreen. After

Ysanne's video played through, I watched it again.

An hour passed. I watched Ysanne over and over, marveling at her delicate face, at the icy transparency of her skin. Her hair was the triumphant yellow of sunset past heavy clouds. The longer I looked at her, the more my conviction grew. She *was* the one I'd been awaiting. I wondered why God didn't confirm it.

Aden returned, dressed in a skin-tight mesh bodysuit over parrot blue tights. I looked up into his face and wondered how old he was: sixteen? Impossible to tell behind the mask of makeup he wore. A royal blue polish had hardened on his eyelashes so that blinking was a slow, painful process. The dust that coated his skin reminded me of the white rice powder the Kabuki dancers used in ancient Japan.

"How do I look?" he asked eagerly.

"Like a china doll."

"Is that a compliment?"

"It was meant to be."

Smiling, Aden handed me a slip of plastic. "This is your ticket." I understood it was a reward for telling him what he wanted to hear.

He summoned his limo via the terminal by the door and drew on a cape of black feathers. He'd worn it in Ysanne's video.

Aden touched my shoulder as I pulled on my leather coat. "Why don't you leave your backpack here, so you won't have to worry about it during the show? I mean, unless you have a place to stay tonight?"

"Thank you."

"Come and go as you like," Aden invited. His green eyes were downcast as he held my palm against the screen for the computer to memorize. "I don't have anything worth stealing, but the video system. If you need money that bad…"

"I don't," I said. I hate it when the arrangements get cozy.

The gilt-bordered mirrors of the lobby highlighted Aden, but my reflection was less flattering. His short black hair was shellacked against his skull, while mine, auburn, was as tangled as Medusa's. I pushed it over my shoulders, shivering. Aden looked very masculine in those blue tights. None of that was padding.

In the twilight, the limo waited in front of the building. I strolled after Aden, wanting to savor the coolness of the air on my face. The breeze reeked of raw sewage and auto exhaust. My eyes burned.

Aden arranged the feathers of his cape around him as the limo glided away from the curb. He slid a chip into the player and Ysanne's voice gathered on the air, almost palpable. She sang that the world was doomed.

"Do you believe in that?" I asked. "The apocalypse?"

Aden didn't know the word.

"Ysanne's prophecy about the end of the world," I supplied.

He closed his eyes. "Ysanne believes it. She's building a spaceship to take us to heaven."

Frowning, I stared at the blackened window. A spaceship? Perhaps I had misjudged Ysanne. It seemed childish to think that the will of God could be escaped. Unless it was God's will that some fled. I hadn't considered that before. He'd allowed Noah to build the ark. Maybe things weren't as hopeless as I'd thought.

We arrived fashionably late. Kids already packed the auditorium. They smelled of formaldehyde, sweat, and cigarettes. Aden immediately saw someone he knew, so I drifted away, trusting we would find each other after the show. I wedged between two doll boys and pushed my back against the wall. The scene took me back. I envied Aden his drugged haze as the waiting began.

A musical phrase trickled from speakers on either end of the hall. Conversation faltered. Suddenly, silence pounded inside my skull until my teeth clenched against her name. I half-expected those around me to fall to the floor and begin speaking in tongues.

At the last moment of sanity, Ysanne walked onstage, her cape reflecting a silver-green nimbus around her. She paused at the stage's edge to survey her congregation, then began to sing.

I'd had religious experiences before. Occasionally I wished to become inured to the voice of God when it spoke of the inevitability of human suffering, of our unavoidable deaths.

Ysanne sang of death: the Earth's, humanity's. No chance, without her. Trust her completely or abandon hope. I slid down to the floor, unable to stand.

I did not see her leave the stage at the show's end. First the auditorium felt achingly empty, then the lights came up on the silent house.

Aden helped me to my feet. Tear tracks marred the perfection of his makeup. A muscular man stood behind him, arms crossed and eyes wary. "One of Ysanne's bodyguards," Aden explained. "He said she wants me at her party tonight. You'll come, won't you?"

I clutched his shoulders and tried to locate my vanished equilibrium. Finally, I nodded. When God summons me, I am unable to resist.

Aden pushed past me into Ysanne's penthouse, propelling me into the party. The collective gaze flashed over me icily. I should have guessed I would be wildly out of place.

Aden put a glass into my hand. It contained a shimmering silver liquid that smelled of licorice and something bitter, like wormwood. His hands were shaking.

"What's wrong?" I asked.

"Ysanne has this effect on me." A shudder danced through him, rattling his bracelets. His smile was dreamy. "I need a poke."

Praying he knew his limits, I kept silent. I liked something about this boy, perhaps his vulnerability. When I looked up from my drink, he had wandered away.

I found a place from which to watch the party. Glowing with innocence, young people clustered around Ysanne. She burned with the compelling halo that I had seen surrounding God. I ached inside, straining to hear the voice. No directive came.

"Have we met?" a woman asked.

Startled out of my meditation, I looked up into Ysanne's eyes. Her lovely face was geometrically perfect: eyebrows, cheekbones, jawline. I couldn't remember anything I had meant to say. "I'm here with Aden."

She smiled, scrutinizing my T-shirt and jeans. Then she

pushed back the white curtains beside me to expose glass doors. "Shall we talk on the balcony?"

Her tone held a challenge. I followed her out. The night wind had cleared some of the pollution. I sucked in a deep breath and felt the claustrophobia fade. I remembered what I had to say. "God has spoken to me, too."

Her lovely, arctic eyes turned to me. "Has He said anything about me?"

Sadness swirled inside of me. "Not in a while."

She looked off over the city. Its lights twinkled in the murk. "Were you disappointed by my concert?"

"No." I longed to touch her as much as I feared to. "Are you the Messiah I've been waiting for?"

Ysanne was quiet a long time. My hopes withered painfully. At last she said, "I did not come to Earth to be worshipped."

She turned my face toward her. Her lips were sweet on mine before she returned to her party. I clutched the plasteel railing for support. The voltage of that kiss made me twitch and twitch again. Aden's drink dropped from my hand and vanished into the distance above the street.

When reality steadied, I let myself back into the apartment. Aden cornered me, his nose wrinkled at the smell that had come inside on my clothing. "How can you breathe out there?"

Without waiting for an answer, he pushed a heavy plastic card into my hand. "That's my limo key. The car's waiting downstairs for you. Just tell it to take you home."

I searched the boy's face. Behind the enamel was a blinding ecstasy that knifed me. "You're staying with Ysanne tonight?"

"She asked me to." His pupils had almost vanished. I wondered what he saw, focused so far inside. Then he touched my face and said, "Please stay at my apartment."

I made the same promise I made to all of them. "For a while."

That satisfied him. He didn't tell me he loved me, but I knew. I wished that was only his addiction speaking.

The limo door opened when I inserted the key. Sighing, I slumped into the black upholstery and tried to think of the last one I stayed with. Her name was…Joy.

My body demanded attention. I hadn't eaten since I'd first seen Ysanne on the video. I hadn't slept in a bed since I left Joy's that same night. I wanted Aden. I wanted Ysanne.

The car announced our destination and opened the door. As I stepped out, I ordered it back to its garage. The limo purred in answer and pulled away from the building.

The lobby, elevator, and upstairs hall were deserted. Filtered air whistled around me, too warm for my coat, more the correct temperature for Aden's mesh bodysuit. I wondered what the other apartments' inhabitants—if there were any—wore.

I placed my hand on Aden's compscreen. The door hummed open and lights flickered on. Without Aden's presence, the place resembled an abandoned hall of mirrors. I set the machine to play Ysanne's video while I scrounged for dinner.

It should have occurred to me that a junkie model wouldn't keep much food. The refrigerator held several cans of diet soda and a pan of something gone furry. In the meat drawer I discovered a couple slices of crusty processed cheese. I broke off the hardest edges, stuffed the rest of the cheese into my mouth, and washed it down with a handful of tap water.

I sank onto the sofa and put my feet up on the coffee table. Aden's used syringe lay beside my leg. Its tiny eye bit my fingertip. I touched the dot of blood to my tongue and found it bitter with the drug.

The videochip halted. Instead of playing the video again, I stumbled off to the bedroom. I had a lot to think over.

I kicked off my boots and left them jumbled with my jeans on the floor. My eyes were bleary with exhaustion. I crawled into the disheveled bed. The sheets smelled of spicy cologne, boyish sweat, and the licorice-wormwood alcohol. I curled around the pillow, both saddened and relieved to be alone. It had been a long time since I'd been immersed in the madness of the city. Smelling Aden, I clutched the pillow and rocked myself to sleep.

Something chirped insistently in the dark room. An alarm, I guessed, struggling to disentangle my legs from the sheets. The clock read 5:14 PM. By the time I realized the sound came from the phone, it quit ringing.

I collapsed back onto the mattress, adrenaline singing through me. Where was Aden?

When I got up to look, his syringe shimmered on the coffee table. I couldn't imagine the Aden I'd observed yesterday separated from his drugs for long. I retrieved my backpack from the doorway and wadded my dirty clothes around a fresh hypodermic and the bottle of pills. He had to still be at Ysanne's. From the terminal, I summoned Aden's limo.

Through the brownish daylight I saw that the concrete facade of Ysanne's apartment building crawled with meticulously sculpted ivy. At first, I marveled at the work, then decided it must have been poured that way. No stonemason would work outside these days.

The limo pulled into the enclosed breezeway. Without Aden to escort me, I shook with nerves. What if the security people wouldn't let me in?

"I'm here to see Ysanne," I told the doorman as I peeled a bill off the wad I'd found in Aden's drug case. The amber-toothed man stared into my face. The money disappeared into his red jacket.

I brushed past him and he tugged a pistol from his waistband. "Ysanne isn't seeing visitors today."

He marched me into an office, pushed me into a folding chair, and pointed his gun at me while the manager punched up Ysanne's apartment on the phone. No one answered. It rang and rang.

As I began to panic, one of Ysanne's bodyguards filled the phone screen.

The doorman nudged me forward with the gun barrel. Words spilled out of me: "I came to Ysanne's party last night with Aden. He never came home. He forgot to take his medicine with him. Is he okay?"

"Wait there," the bodyguard answered. "We've been trying to reach you. I'll come down."

He was ugly in the way of muscular men. His heavy face

seemed molded of half-congealed chicken gravy, but his brown eyes glittered with appraisal. I hoped he didn't like what he saw.

He escorted me—my skin crawling—to Ysanne's door. Instead of grabbing me, he reached past my shoulder to put his hand over the lockscreen, then followed me into the penthouse.

Red sunlight flooded through the picture window. Ysanne stood silhouetted against the glass. "Who's that?" she asked without turning.

"That friend of Aden's."

The smell of spilled liquor made my stomach clench. Bottles littered the floor, especially around the window. At this moment, Ysanne seemed only a woman. It looked as if Aden had hurt her. I wondered if I shouldn't have come. "I worried when I woke up alone."

"Aden is dead."

The cold tone of her voice rocked me. "How?"

"OD, they said." Ysanne took a long hard drink from the bottle in her hand. "I woke up beside his corpse this afternoon." She pitched the bottle at the nearest wall. It hit with a thump, spattering quicksilver droplets.

Ysanne scooped another bottle off the floor and threw it after the first. Then she threw a third.

"Stop."

She stared at me. I felt her iced blue stare through the dusk. Ysanne bent to pick up another bottle.

I crossed the room to her. "Stop, dammit. Stop. You don't need to prove to me you loved him."

"Is that what I'm doing?"

"You weren't throwing bottles before you had an audience."

The bottle dropped from her hand. "Fine," she said and waved the bodyguard away.

Ysanne slopped some silver liqueur into a glass. "Who are you?" she demanded. "You were all Aden talked about last night. He didn't even know your name."

She stumbled and I barely caught her. She kissed me, missing my mouth, and sloshed her drink against me. It burned through my T-shirt.

"What is that stuff?"

"I brought it from home." She offered me what was left in the glass, but I shook my head.

I guided her over to one of the low white sofas. Silence pressed against me, smothering.

"Who are you, Ysanne?"

She sucked the gray syrup from her glass. "My people believed they were Chosen by the Lord of Creation. But the Lord destroyed our world, weeding out disbelievers with plagues, then with famine. In our quest for a new home, we discovered your planet and recognized the same patterns which destroyed ours. My companions continued their search, but I volunteered to rescue those I could. I'm failing." She stared at me with those large, frozen eyes. "Because there's so little time left, humans believe they have license to do whatever they can before they die."

We both thought of Aden.

I broke the silence once more. "Did God tell you when the end would come?"

She made a strangled noise that I realized was laughter. "Look around. This is the end. You're the first human I've met who voluntarily breathes the outside air. Yet the others refuse to give up their automobiles. They're unable to build aboveground any longer. They're unable to farm. Soon they'll be unable to leave their homes. How long after that will civilization survive?"

So I'd been right. The end was at hand, but Ysanne offered deliverance. My quest was over. What should I do now that I'd found the Messiah? How could I serve her?

As she passed out on her feet, the bottle slipped from her hand. I dodged forward to right it before much of the liquor splashed out.

When I lifted her, she didn't rouse enough to put her arms around my neck. Her long limbs dangled, snagging the furniture. Luckily for me, she was as light as a child.

The domed gray ceiling of her bedroom echoed my footsteps. A single tube of blue neon hung suspended above the enormous bed. Like the rest of the apartment, the room reeked of wormwood and licorice.

Beneath the voluminous robe, Ysanne's flawless skin was

paper-white. She seemed as perfect as a crystal bell, so fragile that she might ring if flicked with a fingertip. As I tucked the black sheets around her, I wondered at her marvelous symmetry. I took it as proof she had truly manufactured this body.

I slipped off my boots and climbed into bed. Ysanne burned warmly in my arms, her halo shining past my eyelids.

If it be your will, I prayed, *show me how to serve her. Let us save what we can of my people.*

I was nearly asleep when God spoke. *You've done so well until now, Beloved,* the voice said. *Why choose to fail me now? They have all forsaken me, every one. There shall be no escape from the will of God.*

When I came back to myself, my tongue was bleeding. I debated ignoring those hard words, even as I retrieved my backpack from the other room. I broke up the drug as I'd watched Aden do, carefully doubling the dosage. The needle glided under Ysanne's alabaster skin. She made a soft sound as the rush hit her. My love for her ached inside me. Her lips tasted of licorice.

After the convulsions, it was over. I wiped my fingerprints from the syringe and the crucible and clenched Ysanne's warm hand around them. My first impulse was to run, but the bodyguard would remember me and the apartment computer would have my image on file. I stripped down to my T-shirt, then snuggled against Ysanne's body, fighting down the lump in my throat. I wished Joy were alive, so there might be someone I could go home to. After the inquest cleared me of Ysanne's death, I'd have to trawl the bars again. Someone would take me home and keep me until God called me once more. Someone always did. That was the only benefit I found in being Beloved.

My tongue throbbed where I had bitten it.

Sound of Impact

One of David's favorite places: that was all he'd tell me about our destination. He bustled me out of his house into his white pickup, one eye on the sky and one hand on my knee, dodging in and out of traffic on Los Feliz, then cranking hard right into the Hollywood Hills.

Before I could catch my breath, we stood shoulder to shoulder on the balcony behind the verdigris-domed Griffith Observatory, gazing down on Los Angeles. Overwhelmed by the megalopolis, I was homesick for pocket-sized San Francisco. I tried to imagine the small quadrant my hometown would cover of the *Blade Runner* grid below us. Yearning, crazed, scared, I had the feeling I was about to break something irreplaceable.

The paint on the Observatory behind us peeled in large graceful curls. David remembered when the paint had last been fresh: 1984, when he moved to LA. I hadn't realized he'd been there so long. We'd met in December 1980. Nearly twenty years later, we were on our first date since high school. We'd known each other almost half our lives. I'd been married most of that time. I wondered what he thought of me, now that sunlight and gravity and an unrepentant sweet tooth had done their dirty tricks. Menopause wasn't far off for me. I wasn't the dark-haired sylph he remembered.

A breeze caressed my skin, lifted his soft blond hair into cowlicks. David had timed our arrival at the Observatory to catch the sunset. More exquisite than any watercolor painting, golden sheets of mist hung above the Santa Monica Mountains, each layer progressively darker. Across the city, a small orange ember sank behind the high-rises downtown.

David turned me around to kiss me. It felt different to kiss someone not my husband outside, where the world could watch.

When the kiss dissolved, we leaned forward over the

balustrade, watching swallows swoop back to their nests below. I'm the sort of person who prefers to walk rather than ride, who likes time to think before I act. That evening, I envied the birds. When you step off into the air and find yourself supported by your wings: that must feel like kissing someone for the first time.

Of course, neither of us spared any thought to how dangerous public affection might be. I was a long way from home and probably safe, but we could've run into someone who knew David or, worse, a friend of his wife's. All I knew is that I *wanted* to kiss him, long and gently, and devil damn anyone who disapproved.

In the park below us, two distant figures and their dogs left the wide dusty road for the privacy of the trees. I smiled.

"What are you thinking?" David asked.

Caught. I stared at him, trying to phrase an evasion. Finally, flustered, I admitted to thinking about having sex outside, a fantasy I'd never had an opportunity to indulge.

David smiled, tracing his index finger down my cheek. His hazel eyes changed color like a stormy ocean, so different from my husband's coffee-brown eyes. I'd known David a long time, so I assumed he wouldn't hurt me. He lived a long way away from my life, so I thought I could keep things separate. I thought, given time, I would gain control of myself.

The sun dropped into the densest layer of color, just above the ocean. The ball of fire glowed the color of a dusty raspberry. Rather than setting, the sun seemed to dematerialize.

"That's so amazing," I sighed.

"It's amazing that it rises again," David interpreted.

"No, it's amazing that it does this same beautiful thing, day after day, whether anyone stops to watch or not. It's not beautiful for our pleasure, but just because it is."

He kissed me because I wasn't making sense.

I clasped him hard against my body, eyes squeezed shut, wanting to smell him and taste him and inhabit this moment forever. I couldn't remember the last time I'd watched a sunset with someone. What a gift: that someone would stage a sunset for me.

The last light reflected in creamy gold from the angular

buttresses of the planetarium. Above and behind it, the sky was peacock blue. I wished I had my camera. A photo would've made a talisman, a souvenir. In future days, I could have gazed at the image and remembered: at this moment I felt perfectly happy.

We climbed the stairs to the roof. The door to the big refracting telescope stood open, so we joined the line. A turnstile counted us off as we entered the sanctuary. Instead of a tidy queue, little groups clustered, chatting in various languages. One by one, each person docilely mounted the wooden steps and leaned toward the eyepiece of the huge telescope. No one spoke to the astronomer sitting in a wheeled desk chair below.

My turn came at last. Through the telescope, I watched a pinpoint of bright white light flare and flicker, throwing out sharp rays of light like an old-fashioned compass rose.

"What are we looking at?" I asked.

Pleased to be noticed, the astronomer answered, "Arcturus."

I wondered why he'd chosen it. Staring up through the slit of the Observatory dome at the deepening dusk, my unaided eye couldn't find the invisible star. Cool, I thought. I'd never examined an actual star before.

Outside the Observatory dome, the wind gusted, colder now, and me without my jacket. Shivering, I joined the stream of people filing down the external stairs to ground level. David caught my hand and pulled me inside the Hall of Science.

He led me to the black closet-sized camera obscura booth. The onrushing night outside the Observatory made a shadow play on a reflective screen at the front of the room. Two preteen boys leaned over it, watching the ghosts of headlights weave up the road to the Observatory.

David drew me toward the back of the cramped booth. He gathered me in his arms and kissed me more passionately than before. I submitted only briefly, too aware of the proximity of the kids. While I fantasized about having sex al fresco, the fantasy did not include an underage audience. I slipped out of David's hands into the little museum.

An exhibit about a woman who'd been struck by a meteorite grabbed my attention. The space rock fell through her roof to nail her as she napped on her sofa. The victim's '50s hairstyle dated the black-and-white photo. She lay on her back, the white sheets opened to reveal a mark larger than a loaf of bread across the white skin of her hip. The injury seemed ominously dark in the photo. A man in doctor's whites stood over her, looking down in posed concern. David spoke for them: "'I don't want you to take a picture of the bruise,' she would say. And his answer would be: 'Think of the money and close your eyes.'"

Something about the casual cruelty of his imagined dialogue gave me pause. I turned away from him and the display, unwilling to confront my discomfort. Nearby, two meteorites rested on low tables where children could touch them. Huge staples pinned them in place. David wondered if people had tried to steal them, despite signs that said one weighed 220 pounds and the other more than 600. I guessed that the staples were meant to hold them in place in case of earthquakes, so 600 pounds of meteorite didn't fall through the floor.

David halted at the exhibit of pictures carried by the *Voyager* space probe. The number of tiny slides was overwhelming, but my attention fastened on the illustration of our internal organs. "It's good," was all I could think to say, "that we're showing them how to kill us."

"I wonder about that picture of sex organs," David said. I had to search for it. Sketched purely in outline, the illustration was so clinical that I didn't immediately recognize what I saw. How could otherworldly lifeforms glean *any* information from that?

The black-and-white photo of birth also confused me. The camera gazed down the woman's body and across the big soft expanse of her belly, toward a masked doctor holding a newborn up by its feet. The squashed baby scowled. The umbilical from its belly disappeared beneath the plane of the woman's body. "Oh, look!" I commented. "They'll know we have parasites."

If you wanted to convey that we give live birth, wouldn't you show a photo of the baby exiting the mother? Of course, these pictures had been collected in the '70s, before *Voyager* was launched. I didn't imagine we were any more progressive or honest about reproduction now.

David and I lingered over the Foucault Pendulum, waiting to see it tip over a domino on the floor. The huge pendulum swung tantalizingly close to its victim. A little boy asked, "If it stops swinging, does that mean the world has stopped turning?" His father didn't answer. Yes, I thought, that's exactly what happens when you fall in love. The world stops. Your brain stops. Everything stops.

Trailing David out of the museum, I shuddered, missing my coat. If David hadn't raced me out of the house, we would've missed the sunset. If he'd told me we were going up on the mountain, he would've ruined the surprise. While he'd known to grab his own coat, he hadn't thought to collect mine. It was another omen that—for him—the gesture was more significant than its consequences. I wondered if that way of life would appeal to me long.

David guided me across the plaza in front of the Observatory. We stopped at the sundial rising in front of Art Deco statues of the astronomers. "Put your hands on the end," he said.

I hesitated. Something about the copper gnomon and its 45-degree angle struck me as too phallic to touch in public. I placed my palms on the base of the cold metal obelisk. David leaned against my back and reached around me to rub my arms.

I snatched my hands away from the sundial and pulled away from him. "What are you doing?"

"Making use of the conductive powers of copper to warm you up."

I rubbed my hip against him for the briefest second and said, "Be careful of that."

Our eyes met. Then I dodged away, toward the parking lot.

He hurried up behind me and caught my hand.

Sex, as charged as we were, was terrible. He couldn't seem to come. He kept pounding into me and pounding into me, long past the point of pleasure. I tried shifting positions, but he kept moving my legs back up into the air. I held out through boredom into discomfort, but when we got to pain, I finally said, "This isn't working."

He kept going, clearly hoping I'd change my mind. "What do you mean?"

"It hurts."

A moment later, he stopped humping me. "Maybe you need some lube."

"We need some sleep," I answered. I wondered if he'd taken Viagra or something. My rejection of him didn't seem to have softened him up any. I wriggled out from under him and curled into a little ball around my hurt.

The pillow against my cheek smelled like his wife's shampoo. I wondered if he'd wash the sheets before she came home. He retreated to the bathroom, where he stayed a suspiciously long time. I fell asleep waiting for him to come back.

The dream—or my memory of the dream—began with the section of the plane into which I was strapped plummeting toward the ground. The nose of the plane had been ripped away. Several rows of empty seats were all that stretched between me and the highway overpasses curling over each other below. I watched cars zipping along the highways. A clear thought rose in my mind: this couldn't be LA?

I wondered if the drivers below had seen the plane explode, if they'd watched other portions of it flaming in the sky, artfully arcing toward earth.

My seat had been over the left wing. The wings were somehow still attached to what remained of the cabin, somehow still catching some kind of lift. They slowed our fall. Some. Not enough.

I was scared beyond words, beyond prayer, but also somehow at peace. I knew I was going to die. I wasn't ready to die, but there seemed to be no escaping it. Screaming had not helped the people yanked out of their seats in front of us. Screaming was not going to save me or even make me feel better.

Instead, I reached for the hand clenching the armrest next to me. My husband wove his fingers between mine. We hung on to each other literally for dear life.

Something about the heat coming off the desert below us

gave the plane's wings a little lift. It changed the angle of our descent enough that instead of dropping straight down, we evened out a bit. Part of the undercarriage struck something. The plane shuddered, groaned like a living thing.

I love him, I thought. I couldn't squeeze my hand any tighter around his. He wouldn't hear my voice through the shriek of wind and metal. Would he ever know how much I'd loved him?

When I woke up, I reached out toward the body lying beside mine in the darkness. A moment later, recognition flooded in. I'd made a terrible mistake.

At least breakfast was everything promised. The Armenian bakery offered pastries like jewelry: shiny and glowing, fresh and warm and perfect. As I licked cinnamon from my fingers, David asked, "Wanna go back up to Griffith Park and see if we can find some secluded spot to make your dreams come true?"

I flushed cold, thinking he meant the plane crash dream. Then I realized he meant our conversation about having sex outside.

"No," I stammered, "that's okay. I haven't been to LA before. I'd kind of like to see some of the sights before I have to go."

His gaze dove from my face back to the blueberry muffin in his fingers. I'm not sure why he thought I'd let him have a second chance at me. That I was up, showered, and dressed before he woke this morning had been more than a subtle hint. Still, I'd really liked him once. We had a day to kill before I had to be at the airport. I hoped we could make the best of it.

"C'mon! It'll be fun. Didn't you want to show me that store that sells bones?"

His face crumpled into something like a smile. I saw that I'd hurt him. I knew that his wife was spending the weekend with her boyfriend and felt sorry he was lonely. But after last night, when I watched him weigh whether he was going to stop fucking me like I asked or pursue his own satisfaction no matter what, I wasn't eager to try to make him feel any better.

We spent the day doing touristy things: shopping on

Melrose, visiting the graves of Douglas Fairbanks and Johnny Ramone. Eventually I grew suspicious that David was delaying our drive to the airport. When I called him on it, he said that he hated waiting in airports. He'd get me there in time, no worries. Then he regaled me with a story of the time he had to run through the airport and bang on the doors of the gangway in order to board his plane.

Of course there was a traffic jam on the way to Burbank. By the time we reached the airport, I itched with nervous sweat. David wheeled the truck into an illegal parking space, threw it into park, and snatched my carryon. "Run!" he barked.

The Burbank terminal was tiny: three gates that led directly onto the tarmac. Outside the building, a line of passengers climbed a rollaway stair to a little jet. I threw my bags onto the conveyer, pulled off my shoes, emptied my pockets.

David grabbed me into a hug that nearly broke me with its desperation. I turned my face from his kiss and whispered, "I've got to go."

A tendon twitched in his jaw when he released me. Then he asked, "You get the bomb tucked away all right?"

"What?" I gasped. "I can't believe you just said that!"

"Have a safe trip." His eyes twinkled as he turned away.

The supervisor at the checkpoint chattered into a walkie-talkie. I trembled, infuriated, unable to believe that David would do that to me: make the least funny joke at the worst possible time. Did he want to guarantee I'd never speak to him again? Was this punishment for rejecting him?

The woman manning the X-ray machine reversed my bags through the scanner, back and forth, back and forth. Neither of them made eye contact with me. I stood there, sweaty, out of breath, in my socks. I watched the line of people boarding my plane grow shorter and shorter. A woman wearing a bulky vest strode over to me, followed by a man in a blue windbreaker.

"This way, please," she said, taking my arm.

The best scenario I could envision would be that they'd let me board the next plane to San Francisco, after they'd made sure there was nothing explosive in my luggage or hidden in my body. I'd have to endure a cavity search, then tell my husband I missed my plane because of David's poor sense of humor. My face flushed with shame.

The doors to the tarmac closed. I heard David laughing behind me, shouting, sounds of a scuffle. I didn't turn to see.

He'd gone mad. He'd clearly gone mad. This being LA, people were raising their cell phones to record the moment. I ducked my head and, furious, let the security people lead me away.

Justice

Where can Andrade be? I run my finger around the rim of my empty glass and stare into the mirror behind the bottles behind the bar. These Earthers imitate us, their dress as black as our moods. But even though I in my rags and Lens in his leathers look interchangeable with the Earthers here, I had trouble persuading Lens to rest a moment. He is angry with himself for letting Andrade disappear.

Something tugs at my sleeve. "Got a cigarette, babe?"

The Earther sees my fingers twitch. Before he can flee, my fist is twisted in his collar, one knuckle in the dirty hollow of his throat. His flesh is slick as I haul his feet off the floor.

"This is a good time to hassle me," I say, but my heart is not really in the threat. "If we were elsewhere, I'd kill you."

"Sorry, sir," he apologizes, raw-voiced, as if I had torn his throat away. I drop him and watch him scurry off.

"Should've wasted him," Lens growls. He turns another page of the newspaper, scowling at the photographs.

I hang my head. Lens is right as usual. No one will respect me if I don't assert myself.

Abruptly Lens shoves the paper at me. A picture shows a body amidst overturned trashcans. Puddles blacker than his clothing shine on the alley floor. My stomach hurts as if someone punched me.

"Read it, Kemmy," Lens urges in an uncharacteristically quiet voice.

The soft, ugly English alphabet mirrors the people. I want off this planet more than I've wanted anything in a long time. I hold the paper toward the light behind the bar.

"Someone killed Andrade for the money he took from the ship," I summarize. This makes me ache to hit something. I liked Andrade best of my crewmates. "The officials caught the man when he tried to spend too much of the money. He told them what he'd done."

"Where is the killer now?" Lens demands.

I scan the article. "Being held for trial."

"Earthers don't begin to understand justice." The stool scrapes back from the bar as Lens stands. He stalks out to the street and I follow. People step out of our way, staring at me to decide whether I am male or female. Lens puffs up with pride at the attention I attract. I am glad he is there to protect me from the mob.

I stumble into Lens when he halts before a blue-clad man with a handgun at his hip. Sensing confrontation, the other humans move away. Smiling politely, Lens says, "We'd like your help to find where a murderer is being kept."

The man tips his head to look up into Lens's black eyes. "In jail, probably."

Lens snaps, "Where?"

The officer's hand drifts over to rest on his gun. He imagines that he moves slowly enough to avoid our notice. "Why do you want to know?"

"We are 'mates of the boy he killed," I say.

"People are murdered every day, kids. If the man is guilty, he'll get what he deserves when he comes to trial." The policeman's gaze traces my cheekbones. He doesn't want us to leave until he's through looking at me. "Out of curiosity," he says, to stall us, "who we talkin' about?"

I close my eyes and remember, "The paper says he's called Joe Blake."

The policeman's eyes focus on Lens. "Blake is the kid that knifed the counterfeiter, isn't he? He's probably on the third floor at the Eighth, under max security. You boys've got nothing to worry about."

"What'd'you mean?" Lens demands. He shakes with anger.

I grab his arm. "Let it go, " I whisper. "We got what we needed."

Lens nods. He knows not to mess with the law on these backworlds, especially over things we don't understand. The cop watches us speculatively as I follow Lens into an alley. We trans back to the ship. Let the cop wonder why we never come out.

Teo looks up from the com-console where he has been waiting for Andrade to call. Teo and Andrade were as close as two halves of the same being. Teo receives the bad news with tears. I've never seen anyone but Earthers cry before. I dig my nails into my palms to stop my hands from shaking.

Lens punches Teo's arm. "You'll feel better after we get justice."

Teo continues to sob. He is pale, shrunken in his blacks. I wonder whether he has caught an Earth disease. Without Andrade to heal him, we will be in trouble.

Lens turns to the reflective viewport to rebraid his ebony hair. He orders, "Locate the 'Eighth' on the city map, Kem. Vengeance will do us all good."

I lean past Teo and allow the computer to taste my fingertips. When it acknowledges me, I punch in Lens's request. Graphs flash by the green screen: Eighth Avenue Lounge, Eighth District Court, Eighth Precinct Jail. I ask for definitions of the last two. Then I link our computer to the one at the jail. After it tells me which cell Blake is in, I fix the correct floor plan in my mind and report.

"Good." Lens twists a black ribbon around the braid, which is as thick as my wrist. He joins hands with me and Teo. Lens takes the destination from my mind and we trans out.

We materialize in a gray concrete corridor. Its walls are interrupted at intervals by steel bars.

"Blake?" Lens asks.

Shockingly pale eyes squint from the cage at us. "What do you want?"

"This." Lens transes in, hauling the human back from the bars with one gloved hand.

"Fuck me," Blake whispers.

Teo and I follow Lens. Blake's cellmate is breathing shallowly, apparently drugged into unconsciousness. Good. No witnesses.

Lens drops Blake, who stumbles into a fighting crouch.

Brown stubble covers his head and surly face. He smells of anger and Andrade's blood. "Who the hell are you?" he demands.

"'Mates of the boy you killed," Lens snarls. "We're here for justice."

Unexpectedly, Blake grins. "The guards let you queers in to rough me up, huh? Well, I got rights."

"Not with us you don't," Lens gloats.

Blake's punch lands in Lens's palm. As Lens's big hand closes, the Earther's fingers crunch. Screaming, Blake crumples to his knees as if worshipping Lens.

Footsteps thud toward us. Teo grabs me and Lens and transes us out.

Lens hugs me when we reach the ship. He traces a finger along my jaw, but his gaze is for Teo. "We didn't have time to teach Blake much," he says. "These backworlders are slow to learn."

"Of course we'll have to go back tomorrow night," Teo says. Rather than excited, he sounds resigned.

Shrugging him off, Lens opens one of the lockers and returns with a syringe, a piece of tubing, the burner. "Another day on-world will give us more time to check the cargo's purity," he says. "Teo, get some dust."

Lens cooks up the cocaine as I tie the tubing around my arm, yanking it tight with my teeth. The Syndicate gladly allows us a fraction of the cargo as our pay, since not many smugglers will bother to run obscure drugs from the backworlds. The big money is in bringing weapons and starship parts out from the central hub. Lens hopes to captain one of those ships when he grows up.

The next night we trans directly into Blake's cell. My head pounds. The precision required to pinpoint our destination strains the link between our minds. We are weakened without Andrade's calm.

Neither of the sleeping forms in the bunk bed is Blake. Teo whispers hopefully, "Maybe he's dead."

Lens laughs. "We were easy on him yesterday."

"Maybe they took him to a medic for his hand," I suggest.

Leaning over the upper bunk, Lens pops the man with his fist and growls, "Where's the infirmary?"

Curses, mostly unintelligible, answer him. Lens hits the Earther again.

"It's downstairs, damn you. Second floor." The man squints against the light at our backs. "Who are you?"

"Bad dream." Lens thumps him again and we trans out. Lens likes dramatic exits.

The medical ward smells of ammonia. The long white room has four inmates, all of whom appear sedated. Lens moves among the cots, danger dancing in his muscular body. He snatches a sheet from one bed.

Blake cracks one eye open, then sucks in a breath and tries to crawl away. He is strapped to the bed and can't move far.

To impress Lens, I haul the Earther forward, snapping the restraints. "Why're you hiding down here?"

Blake holds up a bandaged hand. "They think I done this to myself. The orderlies been keepin' an eye on me, so don't try anything," he advises.

"Maybe we should take you somewhere else," Teo threatens from over my shoulder. "Leave you in an alley like you left Andrade?"

"Fuck you, faggot. He never shoulda touched me." Even though his unbandaged hand shakes, Blake's voice is steady. I admire that.

Lens pulls Blake out of my grasp. "Why did you kill Andrade?"

"He touched me, offered me money…"

"Don't flatter yourself, Earthman." Teo spits on Blake's white gown. "Andrade only wanted pleasure. If you'd said no, he probably would've given you the money anyway. You killed him for nothing."

Pale with anger, Teo transes one of Andrade's laserknives into his hand. "Let's kill him now and be done."

"No," Lens says. "For Andrade. Wait 'til the Earther realizes what he's cost us."

Each reference to "Earther" has upset Blake more. Now he

stares at the laser, certain that it wasn't in Teo's hand before. He is beginning to think that we only look human, to recall that we walked through his walls last night.

"Guards," Blake sobs. The sound is somehow caught in his throat. "Guards."

A slow smile spreads across Lens's face. "Don't make us give you something to whine about," he advises, lifting Blake out of bed. He drops the Earther to the white floor and gives him a kick so sharp that I hear ribs crack. Lens kneels and yanks the Earther's face to within a hand's breadth of the metal cot frame. "Did you kill Andrade for the money?"

"No. I took that afterwards."

Lens slams Blake's head down against the sharp metal edge. A line of blood appears along the man's forehead. His unbandaged hand twitches, but he does not yell.

"You killed him because he touched you?"

Blake mumbles, "Yes."

His head slams down again.

"Did you ever kill anyone before?" Teo asks.

"No," Blake gasps. "And I didn't mean to kill him!"

Lens shoves his head down again. "You're rationalizing."

"No, I mean it." Tears glisten at the corners of Blake's swelling eyes. "I just cut him and grabbed the money and ran. I thought someone would find him before he bled to death..."

Teo ignites the laserknife. "I've heard enough."

"Keep watch," Lens snarls. "I'm not done."

Furious, Teo stalks off. I look between the two, then follow Teo. "What's the matter with you?" I ask. "Andrade was your pair. You owe him justice."

"What Lens is doing isn't for Andrade anymore, if it ever was. Andrade wouldn't want this." Teo's voice is shrill, unfamiliar. "Fuck traditional justice."

The words sound strange coming from him. Teo is the only person I know with a traditional pair-bond. At least, he was. It takes me a moment to recover. "Think of it as soothing Lens's conscience," I say. "He shouldn't have allowed Andrade off the ship without you in the first place."

"Forget it, Kemmy." Teo's gaze is a frozen gray. "You don't

understand."

"So tell me." I pull Teo around to face me. "What don't I understand?"

"You've never been in love. You don't even like us much, but Lens and the things he gets away with fascinate you. You're only a child, Kemmy. If you're not careful, someone will kill you because of it, like they killed Andrade."

I can only stare at him. Finally Lens calls us back. When he rolls Blake onto the cot, the human's face looks like shredded meat.

"Now that he's dead, can we get off this rock?" I beg. I've had enough of smugglers for a while. I hope I can find another crew when we get home. Explorers, maybe. Something legal.

The harsh light catches in Blake's eyes, which are blue as his sky.

"He's not dead," Teo says flatly.

"No," Lens gloats. "Tomorrow we'll kill him. Let him be afraid first."

"Enough!" Teo leaps forward, the knife ignited.

I know Lens, what he will do. I dodge between them. Lens's gaze drills into my eyes, his fist drawn back to strike. I wonder if he is the one Teo thinks will kill me. I trans the laser from Teo's hand into my own. I will cut Lens if he moves. He knows it. With an infuriating smile, he drops his arm.

Then he transes us out. When we reach the ship, Lens slaps me into the wall. Before I shake my head clear, Lens is on Teo. Both of them are screaming about killing Blake.

My limbs feel paralyzed, as if nothing I can do will stop this insanity.

Teo gasps for breath. No time to think. I leap onto Lens's back, trying to pull him away. Over his shoulder I see Teo's face turn blue.

Between clenched teeth, Lens snarls, "Get off me, Kemmy, or I swear you're next."

"Let him go!"

"Teo's already dead."

Lens stands up, throwing me easily to the deck. My head hits hard. Lights flash before my eyes. Lens bends to kiss me. "Are you okay?" he asks as he takes the laser from my limp fingers.

I nod. There is blood in my mouth. When I look over, I see Teo's caved-in throat. I stagger to my feet.

"After we take care of Teo's body," Lens says, "we'll go back to the jail and finish off Blake. I think you're right, Kemmy. We gotta get off this rock." He lifts Teo's shoulders and I take his feet. We dump him outside the ship in the warehouse where the ship is hidden. It is likely that no one but rats will ever find the body.

Much later Lens is sleeping. I cannot. I think about killing Lens to get revenge for Teo. But I cannot fly the ship alone. There might be other smugglers on this world, but I wouldn't be able to recognize them. They'd look Earther, just like us. My body trembles uncontrollably. I understand, now, what fear is.

Andrade died because he trusted everyone. Teo died protesting tradition. I want to kill my only escape off this planet because of a stupid Earther ideal called friendship. All because they have two sexes on this damn planet, rather than one. Andrade and Blake and Teo had to die because we misunderstood all that meant.

To think I believed in justice when we came here.

The Magic of Fire and Dawn

In the deepening twilight, the glade drew inward like a drawstring purse. The glow of the cooking fire reflected in Ardis's necklace of dowry coins. She ladled rabbit stew into a wooden bowl. Her father Sepp accepted his dinner hungrily.

Above the clearing, the sky was purple with impending night. Through the trees, the west glowed violent orange. Ardis bent over the second fire in the clearing, the ritual fire, with a bucket of water. The embers of the sun-fire sparkled the same orange as the sunset. As the girl doused the coals, steam boiled around her. Then it was night.

Ardis returned to the cooking fire. The stew's fragrance tempted her mouth, but her nervous stomach made eating seem foolish. Still, the man had not come and the day of danger was over. It seemed forever since, by the dawn-fire, Ardis had a vision of a man with curling black hair and a fiddler's long fingers. She filled a bowl and settled on the quilt, covering her ankles with her cerulean skirt.

Sepp bolted to his feet, tumbling his stew bowl into the grass. Then Ardis too heard the hoofbeats on the road beside their wagon.

The black horse whickered to the family's pair as it entered the circle of firelight. A tall man swung off its back, his ebony cape swirling around him like the forest wind.

"What do you want, stranger?" Ardis's father asked.

"I come with the greetings of my people." Though he towered over Sepp, the stranger was as thin as a shadow in the cooking fire's glow. Tousled black hair drooped over sable eyes. He pushed it back with long slim fingers. Fiddler's fingers. Ardis wished that she had told her father about the vision.

A shiver ran down her spine as the man pulled a violin from behind his saddle. With a grin, Sepp returned his knife to the wide belt around his belly. Ardis had not even seen him draw it.

"Get the stranger some dinner, Ardis," Sepp said, admiring

the fiddle as the man tethered his horse. Ardis dished up more stew, staring into the bowl as she tried to steady her hands.

"Thank you, Ardis," the man said in a soft voice. "I'm called Morlen."

"Share the safety of our glade for the night, Morlen," Sepp answered.

"Thank you." Morlen folded his legs under him and spooned up the stew. His fiddle gleamed on a fold of his cape. Ardis refilled her father's bowl. The wasted stew lay blackly in the trampled grass at his feet. When everyone had finished, Ardis collected the bowls and scrubbed them clean with sand.

The fiddler tuned his instrument. He waited for her to settle on the quilt again before beginning to play. Morlen hugged the fiddle to his shoulder with his chin. Only his bow arm moved at first, gently caressing the strings, until his entire body swayed. Ardis imagined herself in an embrace as passionate as the fiddler's and blushed.

Slowly the mood of the music changed. It spoke of hollow sadness, a melancholy that dragged at the senses as the earlier tune had fired them.

Ardis roused herself with difficulty, as if from a spell. Dawn would again be late if she didn't get to bed. As the wagon door closed behind her, Ardis thought she heard Morlen wish her pleasant dreams, but it must have been the wind. The music continued without pause.

When she started awake, Ardis heard only her father's breathing. She rolled to face the wagon's center, squinting at the shadowy herbs drying overhead, her father in the big bed, the jumble of his clothing on the floor. It must be very late.

Low music came suddenly, prowling outside the wagon. Ardis felt her heart echo the fiddler. Her feet swung to the floor, summoned to the dance. She pulled her skirt over her chemise, lacing it quickly. Around her waist she wrapped the leather belt her father had made for her, dangling its leather pouches of herbs and tinderbox. Finally, opening the trunk under her cot, she lifted out a shawl of lamb's wool to muffle her dowry coins.

When she stepped out of the wagon, Morlen grinned from

the far side of the glade, his eyes momentarily red as embers. "Did my music wake you?"

"Yes." Ardis crouched beside the coals of the cooking fire. The shadows caressed Morlen. Ardis wondered why she saw him so poorly in the ember-light.

"Why do you have two fire pits?" Morlen asked, polishing his fiddle with a soft cloth.

"One is for cooking," Ardis said. "The other is a ritual fire."

"You light it at dawn and douse it at sunset?"

Her father had warned her never to discuss the ritual with anyone. Ardis did not want to answer, but somehow Morlen compelled her. "Yes."

Morlen smiled as he put the fiddle back into its wrappings. "Come ride with me," he said. Out of the woods stepped his horse. Morlen offered the girl his hand.

Ardis stared at the black hairs that washed down from under his shirt cuff. His thin fingers summoned hers and set her on the horse. She did not resist. He climbed up behind her.

The horse stepped out of the clearing onto the dusty road. Morlen draped his cape over Ardis's shoulders. His warmth fired her flesh.

I cannot ride off alone with a stranger, she thought. Before she could protest, her eyes closed against the shifting pattern of moonlight through the branches. Sometime later she roused, hearing the horse's legs swish against the undergrowth of the forest. Morlen must have guided them off the road. She stared around in alarm.

How could the horse find its way in the blackness? Ardis could no longer see the horse's head, yet the animal traveled so fast that Ardis felt her hair thrash against Morlen's shoulder. Magic, her thoughts whispered.

Straining until her eyes ached, Ardis finally saw the trees ahead silhouetted by a green glow. She expected it was a will-o'-the-wisp, but the light grew until the horse burst through the underbrush into a clearing. A green fire roared in its center.

People bustled around the glade, bridling horses. Hounds tumbled and snapped playfully at one another. A man in black armor stood beneath an oak tree, overseeing the chaos. His face was hidden beneath a helmet with antlers as broad as the king stag of the forest.

Morlen dismounted and held Ardis in his arms a moment. Her toes brushed his shins. She was blushing when he set her down.

"She is the one, your highness," Morlen said as he knelt before the armored man.

Ardis straightened the necklace on her thin chest before she faced the man, trying to exude confidence instead of confusion. Her people had never bowed to kings, her father told her. Nor would she.

Instead of chastising her, the knight unbuckled the chinstrap of his antlered helmet. He lifted the helmet from his shoulders and cradled it in the crook of one arm. Unlike Morlen, this man had hair as pale as yellow field flowers. With eyes innocent and brown like a deer's, he was as beautiful as any lady Ardis had seen at a country fair. She nearly fell into a curtsey out of awe.

"So you are Ardis, daughter of Sepp. Be welcome among my people."

She hesitated, her lips wanting to call him lord. Instead, she answered simply, "Thank you."

A diminutive aide with bowed legs scurried up to the blond man and announced, "The horses are ready, Your Majesty."

Ardis peered at the knight, but he wore no crown and held himself without the rumored arrogance of the English kings. Perhaps he had religious power, she decided. Ardis understood little of the native religion.

"Let us ride," the knight decreed. He replaced the horned helmet on his head.

As the encampment mounted around them, Ardis asked Morlen, "Where are they going?"

He led the way back to his horse. "On the hunt."

"In the dark? Me as well?"

Morlen grabbed her around the waist and hefted her up. Glinting teeth filled his smile. "The dark is the only time to hunt."

He leapt up behind her. The horse sprang forward, plunging through the confusion of the camp to stand beside the horned knight.

"Are you ready, fiddler?" his master asked.

"Ready, Your Majesty!" Morlen struck his heels against the horse's ribs. It leapt forward. Ardis wished she could tear her skirt so she could straddle the horse, for she feared that she would tumble to her death. She was grateful that Morlen's arms circled her.

The hunters raced through the trees and regained the road. The horses' hooves struck blue sparks from the stones. Ardis was glad it was early summer. Had it been autumn, the forest would surely have caught fire.

They slowed at the outskirts of Rushton, where lately Ardis's father spent his days smithing. The streets of the village were deserted at this hour. Morlen slid off the horse and flung his cape over his shoulders. The waning crescent moon cast his shadow to the street. He drew the fiddle from its wrapping, plucked the strings and adjusted their tuning. Then, taking his bow, he played the tune that had summoned Ardis from the wagon.

Once more the music tugged at her feet. Ardis clutched the horse's mane, fighting the sorcery. The villagers, however, heeded the violin's call. One by one, the townspeople wandered from their beds as if still deep in sleep. In these last hours before dawn, they were probably about to wake with the cock's crow to begin their days.

A mournful horn sounded in counterpoint to the violin. The dogs began to whine. The townsfolk woke slowly, rubbing their eyes, shivering in the night air. To Ardis, they looked silly in their night bonnets.

"Will they come with us dressed like that?" she asked. Playing on, Morlen smiled and did not open his eyes.

One of the riders whooped and the hounds charged. A woman screamed, clutched her chemise around her, and began to run. The pack swarmed over her. A dog howled in triumph, its muzzle wet and black in the moonlight. Screams and shouts and baying filled the night. The horsemen charged after the fleeing townsfolk.

Her throat choked, Ardis managed to ask, "You hunt people?"

"Those are the damned. They've turned their backs on Faery ways, and Faery on them." Morlen put the fiddle away and climbed up behind her. Then he kicked the horse into a gallop.

Ardis remembered flashes of what followed. Incoherent images caught behind her eyelids: a child in a tree, the huntsmen gibbering as they summoned green flame. A proud hound carrying a severed hand in its mouth. The horned knight striding through the underbrush, the sword in his hand streaked with blood. And Morlen played his fiddle.

For the first time in her life, it no longer mattered to Ardis that this was not her homeland, that these were not her people. Whether or not they were damned, she wept for them.

As she cried, something featherlike brushed her cheek. She looked upward, seeking a bird. Instead, thick white snowflakes drifted down, melting as they touched her face.

Ardis shivered as she wiped the tears away. It was early summer; the snow should long have been gone. Her thin shawl captured her body's warmth but could not hold it against the wind's increasing bite. Morlen wrapped her in his heavier cape.

The horns sounded another call and Morlen urged his horse toward them. His face, like her own, was turned upward.

With all the authority she could muster, Ardis said, "You must take me back to the wagon soon."

He grinned at her. "I've taken you as wife, little girl. Isn't it the way of your people that the wife goes to live with her husband's folk?"

Ardis was not charmed by his words. Her responsibility rested heavily on her. "I need to light a fire. It doesn't need to be large, but morning will never come if I don't."

He turned her face to him with slim, cool fingers. "Now that you've joined the Hunt, you needn't light the sun-fire again." His words stunned her. "The Hunt only rides at night. We can't collect souls in daylight. Now that you're with us, nothing need distract us from our task."

The huntsmen began to regroup, riding back toward their encampment. Ardis did not want to argue with Morlen in their hearing. She wished she disliked his warmth at her back.

Frost sparkled on the metal fittings of the black horse's bridle when they arrived in the clearing. Ardis's breath clouded the air. The night had grown too cold for snow. As soon as her feet touched the ground, she examined the grass, which snapped off in her fingers.

The huntsmen gathered in a ring to ignite their green fire. Ardis glanced up, but no beam of sunlight pierced the blackness. She considered running, but a goat-headed man squatted nearby, threatening her with his golden eyes.

Startled, she stared at the other members of the Hunt. Although she had assumed they were human, very few seemed so now that she actually looked. Some had floppy ears, or their noses were long and red. Some wore pointed yellow caps pulled low over their misshapen skulls. Others, more beastlike, wore rags. These tended the hounds and gathered firewood, servants of their more human-seeming masters. Ardis had not known so many races lived in England. She had never seen folk like these at the country fairs.

A dwarf scuttled out of the woods, followed by a monster with a froglike mouth. They shuffled up to stand at the feet of the Huntmaster.

"Frozen in their beds," the dwarf proclaimed. "Curled together and rimed with ice."

The frog-creature rolled its bulging eyes.

"How many houses did you search?" the Huntsman asked.

"Seven, as commanded," said the dwarf. "I wanted to check the farmer's house outside of Whitestone Village as well, but Granogh insisted we report to you first."

Ardis felt the cold congeal within her bones. People were dying because she had not summoned the sun. She had to escape. She had to light the sun-fire. It occurred to her that her own father might lie frozen in the old wagon. Tears left trails of ice on her cheeks. The coins of her necklace chilled her through the summer gauze of her chemise.

"Here, my love," Morlen said, startling her. She scrubbed a hand across her face before she turned to him.

The fiddler handed her a steaming mug of mulled wine. The vapor burned her eyes, so she feared to drink from the earthenware cup. She warmed her hands around it instead.

"Did they say people were freezing to death?" she asked. Effort alone kept her voice calm.

"Only the damned will freeze." Morlen shrugged. "You needn't worry."

Wrapping his caped arm around her, he guided her to a pavilion of violet canvas. He ushered her in. "Welcome to your bridal chamber."

Even inside the enclosure, their breaths made mist. Morlen ran cold fingers under her hair, exposing her cheek to his chapped kisses. Warmth she wished she did not feel blossomed through her. She must not take Morlen as her husband. People were dying because she had allowed him to seduce her away from her duty. She held that thought beneath her clenched eyelids and wondered how to escape.

Morlen's fingers brushed her throat, jingling the coins of her dowry necklace. Forcing a smile, she lifted the necklace over her head. "This is yours now," she said, holding the gold coins toward him. After a moment, she added, "Husband."

His eyes glittered, as she had seen other men's eyes glitter when they encountered the dowry. When Morlen reached for the necklace, Ardis used a trick her father had taught her, knotting the chain around his fingers, and ducked out of the tent.

Everyone seemed busy elsewhere, so Ardis fled into the woods. She could not hide from the hounds, so she ran, as hard and fast as she dared. Away from the encampment's fire, the woods were black as a cave.

A dog cried mournfully. The icy air was sharp in her throat. She did not doubt that she was damned by Faery and would be torn to bits by the hounds. Still, she ran. If foreign gods had damned her, let their minions give chase.

She heard Morlen shout her name, his voice full of rage. Ardis wondered why he didn't fiddle her back to the Hunt. Perhaps her trick had damaged his fine fingers. She smiled at that. Then he called for the Hunt to ride and her smile disappeared.

Ardis held out her arms to warn her of trees, but they were no protection from the underbrush. Something tangled in her skirt and pulled her to the ground. Her breath whooshed out. She heard hoofbeats amidst the yowling of hounds. A green torch sparkled among the trees. The Hunt was almost upon her.

Fumbling with the drawstring of her pouch, Ardis pulled out her tinderbox. She marveled that they had allowed her to keep it, but they must have assumed she used spells to light the fire as they did.

She had no idea what sort of grass she lay in, but it felt as if the cold had killed it. She struck the flint against the stone, but the spark faltered in the knifing wind. With no time to curse, Ardis bent forward, using her body as a windbreak. She struck another spark with numb fingers. The grasses glowed a faint red. The wind dropped a little. Ardis peered around for twigs. Without rising, she gathered what she could, careful not to expose the fragile spark. The sticks nearly smothered the ember, but Ardis blew on it slowly, gently, steadily.

Behind her, the Hunt seemed to hold its breath. Ardis dug the herbs from her pouch and added pinches to the flames. Gradually it became easier to see, as if the sun—frozen in its bed during the too-long night—now struggled to rise.

A single horse crashed through the underbrush to stand in the fragile pre-dawn light. The Huntmaster removed his helmet, his eyes aflame with a feral glow.

"Well done, Ardis, daughter of Sepp. Morlen had persuaded me that you were ours, but trickery freed you after all." His smile terrified her more than had the baying hounds.

"Know this," he said. "You will have a daughter someday. As long as your line continues, Morlen will await his bride. Remember that the Hunt is as eternal as night itself."

He wheeled his horse back into the woodland. Ardis turned to the fire to warm her hands before she dug a ring around the flames in the frozen earth. The day would be long indeed if she allowed the forest to catch fire.

A single beam of sunlight slanted through the bare branches in the east. From somewhere in the woods came a man's cheer. Ardis's heart filled with joy as she recognized the voice.

"I'm here, Father!" she called. "I'm here and it's morning."

Still Life with Shattered Glass

As he handed me a beer, Jacob asked, "Shall I introduce you around, Sherry? Or would you rather just *watch* the party?"

He knew I hated Corona, but it amused him to act cool and superior, as if the fact that he was a grad student and I was only a junior altered the fact that he was a poseur. I suspected we wouldn't be together much longer.

I pulled the key chain from my jeans pocket and opened the beer. Without asking, Jacob took my keys and popped open his own bottle.

A woman arrived at Jacob's shoulder. Her mass of permed blond hair draped artfully around the shoulders of a little black dress. "I brought my portfolio," she said, pushing a large black book at him. Without an introduction or excuse, Jacob walked her over to a quieter corner of the room. Their backs made it clear I was not welcome.

Typical. Jacob's friends always come before me.

I turned to look over the rest of the party. The people all seemed to be art students like Jacob, dressed in black and tragically hip. Same old, same old.

Their Business of Art professor's house was nice enough. Under track lighting, well-placed canvases hung on storm-gray walls. Jacob had told me that this professor bought student art, then arranged connections so that, as his protégés became successful, his private collection increased in value. We'd argued about it, in fact. I said the professor had a good scam, that if he gave a damn about his protégés, he'd buy their art after its value increased. Jacob said I was naive.

Later in the evening—several glasses of wine and no sign of Jacob later—I drifted into the lull of the dining room. On the polished granite table rested the blond woman's portfolio. I lifted its cover, expecting to see her in a variety of modeling poses, maybe nude shots. It hadn't occurred to me that the book might contain her photography, that such a beauty was herself an artist.

The first pictures, blurry and uncentered, seemed as if they had been done by a child. The subjects ranged from a butterfly squashed against a Chevrolet's grill to a cluster of fish gutted on a lakeshore. The following pages held several angles of a Siamese cat, dead by the roadside. In the final frame of the series, a fly washed its hands in the blood trickling from the cat's mouth.

"Are you shocked?" a woman asked.

Embarrassed to have been caught spying, I looked up to find the blond in the Aubrey Hepburn dress. I wanted to say something to redeem myself. "They're fascinating. Memento mori, almost."

She flashed a polished white smile. "Composition is the important thing. If you can't make a shot satirical or seductive, it isn't art."

The speech sounded rehearsed, like something she hoped to be quoted on. Fine, I thought. I can play the art game. "How did you choose death as a subject?"

"In terms of still-life, everything else has been done."

I nodded, conceding she'd won. Then my gaze caught on a photograph above the buffet. I moved closer. In the 16x20, a freshly dressed deer hung from a tree, its entrails steaming in the snow beneath it. The name Lily had been scrawled across the scarlet mat.

"That's mine," she said behind me. "Lily Crowe."

I took her hand, gave her my name. So the professor had picked her as up-and-coming. I'd had too many glasses of pinot to fight down a smirk.

"What's your major, Sherry?" Lily asked.

"Theater."

She regarded me critically, her head tipped at an angle. "You've modeled for Jacob, haven't you? I recognize you from his paintings."

Before I could respond, a man called from the living room. "Lily, are you recording the local news?"

"No." She left the room abruptly. I trailed behind her.

Someone turned up the television. "...stumbled between the automobiles stopped at the State Street railroad crossing. He ignored the lowered crossing gate and, apparently, did not hear the warning bells or train's whistle. The engineer told police that he braked the instant he saw someone on the tracks. Even so, the train couldn't stop until two thousand feet after impact."

Channel Four showed only the anchorman reading his script, no scene-of-the-action film. Maybe there hadn't been enough of the victim left to record.

Lily's hand closed on my forearm. "Damn. I didn't record that."

"I think I got it for you." A balding, middle-aged man crouched in front of the TV, fiddling with the electronics until the announcer flickered back on to repeat, "two thousand feet after impact."

"Thanks," Lily said as she accepted a DVD. "Anybody want to go down to the tracks to see if we can find a finger?"

I gasped, "What?"

Her hand was hot on my arm. "If the train took 2000 feet to stop, the body would be shredded. Depending on how finely ground he was, the police *must* have missed something. Let's see what we can find."

"What will you do if you find anything?" I envisioned rows of formaldehyde jars, in which she kept souvenirs of her shoots.

She laughed. "Photograph it."

No one else expressed interest in prowling around the November night. "Most of them are too drunk to be any help, anyway," Lily confided. Jacob appeared from nowhere to hand me my leather jacket.

"Aren't you coming?" I snapped.

He brushed a hand against his raw silk slacks. "I'll pass."

The expedition reminded me of the beginning of *Blue Velvet*. While I wasn't sure I wanted to see anything like that in real life, I really had nothing better to do.

State Street was deserted, probably until the bars closed. I was relieved no one would see us behaving like ghouls. Lily parked at the produce market beside the train tracks. "There's a flashlight in the glove box." She lifted a camera bag from the trunk.

I swallowed hard, my mouth dry despite the aftertaste of pinot. "I've never seen a dead body before."

"Relax. You won't see much of one tonight."

I followed her across the street, glad to have my Docs on in case I stepped on anything. Lily scanned the tracks exhaustively, barely gaining ground. When I could stand the silence no longer, I asked, "How'd you get into this?"

"You mean, what made me 'like this'?" A smile colored her voice in the darkness. "What incident in my unfortunate childhood made me such a pervert?"

When I didn't answer, she laughed at me. "Maybe my brother made me pose naked and shared the pictures with his friends. Maybe my parakeet died and I kept her in a shoebox under my bed. Maybe my father took me out to the barn to watch him butcher rabbits. What do you think?"

I batted the question back to her. "What do *you* think?"

Her smile reflected the flashlight. "I don't think about it."

We scoured a good length of track before Lily decided, "They must have gone over this area with dogs."

I changed the subject, hoping to cheer her up. "What do you plan to do with your photographs?"

"I'd like to get into the collection at the Detroit Institute of Art. And Professor Richardson, at the party tonight? He's helping me find a book publisher."

Do you find enough subjects? I wondered. What happens if the deadline looms and no body parts turn up? Ann Arbor is a small town. It couldn't have that many violent accidents, could it?

As we drove back to the party, I wondered how someone could ignore the warning gates and bells. What does one feel as the train barrels down the track? I hoped the agony had been quick, that he hadn't regretted it.

Jacob had disappeared from the party. Someone familiar, another painter whose name I couldn't recall, said Jacob left with a sculptor. I nodded, clutching my calm front. On the couch, Lily chatted with her professor. I wondered if she had been another of Jacob's distracter techniques—an accomplice to get me out of his way for the evening—but that was paranoid. The whole finger hunt scheme was too elaborate for Jacob. He'd merely taken advantage of the situation.

And he was a genius at that. The space on the street where I'd parked my car was empty. I stood there, stupidly checking the landmarks to make sure I was in the right place. Then I remembered giving Jacob the bottle opener, my keys still attached, to open his Corona. I stared at the pavement, too angry to think.

"Has your car been towed?" Lily asked.

I didn't know where she'd come from, but I was in no mood to be civil. "Jacob borrowed it to take home a 'friend'."

"He'll be back for you, won't he?"

"I doubt I'm on their minds at the moment."

She let that go. "I can give you a ride."

"Don't worry about it," I said. "Jacob's got my apartment key, too. He won't let me in." I took a deep breath to fight the constriction in my chest. "I've got friends on North Campus I can crash with. It's getting to be a regular Friday night thing."

"Roommates can be a drag," Lily said.

There was a world of sympathy in her voice. I realized I didn't want to walk to North Campus. "Do you have a sofa?" I asked.

"The most comfortable sofa in the world."

"Can I borrow it?"

The moment she walked into her apartment, Lily switched on a police scanner. Jacob could not live without background noise either, but at least he settled for punk shows on WCBN.

An invitingly long sofa shared Lily's living room with a television and a jumble of DVDs. A laptop and a DVR nestled on the TV stand. Lily slipped the new DVD out of her coat pocket and onto the pile. As I glanced over the labels, I saw that most compiled news clips.

The police scanner crackled and a voice ordered paramedics to a bar on the edge of town, where a bouncer had been knifed.

I began to lace my boots back up when Lily asked, "Going somewhere?"

"Don't you want a picture of that?"

Her smile told me it was a dumb question.

"Okay." I leaned back, laces dangling. "Why not?"

"He won't die. The ambulance will be there before we get to the car. I only photograph fatalities." She stretched, as if to allow me to enjoy the way the black dress slithered over her curves. "After poking around in the dirt, I need a shower. Want to join me?"

I was still pissed at Jacob, so I said, "Sure."

She sent me in to get started while she took off her makeup. I shucked my clothes and left them on the bathroom floor, where they'd be easy to find later.

My mind wasn't on Lily at all as I stood in the shower and let the water beat on my skull. It was November. My name was on the lease until May. What the fuck was I going to do about Jacob?

The lights in the bathroom went out.

"Hey!"

The shower door slid open. "You ever take a shower in the dark?" Lily asked.

"No." I backed into the corner. The ceramic tile was chilly. The bathroom was as dark as a coffin. Nobody knew I'd come home with her. What if I just vanished?

Lily closed the shower door behind her. Her hand found my shoulder. She wore a latex glove that reached to her elbow. "The darkness makes perspective impossible," she purred, drawing me into her latex-sheathed arms. "Is there anywhere I can't touch you?"

"No," I repeated, pulling her head to meet my kiss. Her tongue forced my lips open as her gloved hands explored me. I braced one foot against the top of the tub while she confirmed that I had no problem being touched.

It was weird not being able to see anything. Had I ever been in such perfect blackness? It could be anyone's hands on my body. The sound of the shower drowned out our movements. I wasn't sure if she was breathing hard. My knees shuddered beneath me.

"If I crack my head on the porcelain, will you take my picture?" I wondered.

"Only if you die," Lily promised. "Are you gonna fall?"

"Maybe," I hedged.

"Then go lie down. There's a drawer in the night table that's full of toys. Why don't you pull out anything that interests you?"

"Can I fuck you?" My voice was lower than usual, but my nerves were reasonably well masked.

"You like to fuck?"

"I liked to fuck Jacob up the ass, the stupid motherfucker."

Before I lost it, Lily leaned in to kiss me. Then she asked, "Did he like it rough?"

I laughed.

"So do I," she admitted. "That purple dildo is my favorite. Why don't you go strap it on? I'll just be a minute."

Her bedroom seemed standard femme, lavender blue comforter flung across the bed, perfume and jewelry scattered atop the dresser. I moved to the nightstand, expecting to find books on bondage or bullfighting. Instead she was reading *On the Genealogy of Morals*.

In the top drawer I found a rainbow of negligees. The silk cradled a handgun, cold under my fingertips, against the lace. Of course she had a gun, I told myself. It had probably been in her camera bag while we looked for the finger. She was a single woman who worked at night. Of course she had a gun.

Heart pounding, I eased that drawer closed and opened the next one. A jumble of sex toys filled it. The handcuffs had a key in one of their locks. They were the cheap kind that they sell in sex shops, but I figured she wouldn't have them if she didn't like them. I tested the key, made sure they opened, and crawled under the covers.

The phone rang, shocking me awake. I couldn't remember where I was. A woman spoke quietly. The voice brought the evening back to me in a rush, starting with the finger hunt.

Lily flicked on the bedside light. When I peeled my eyes

open, she was combing her fingers through her hair. "I'm going on a shoot," she said. "If you want to come, get dressed. I have to be there now."

Except for the glow of the streetlights, South University Street was vacant. The bars must have closed. I squinted groggily at my phone. 3:57 AM.

Lily pushed open the chain-link gate to the alley behind the University Towers apartment building. The sharp intake of breath made me wonder what could shock her. I forced myself to follow.

An overhead flood lit the alley, glinting off a rack of chained bikes. Lily attached the flash to her camera.

At her feet sprawled a body. The girl's black eyes stared past Lily at the stars overhead. Straight black hair fanned out on the pavement like a satin blanket thrown across the pool of blood. The back of her skull was flattened. I leaned against the cold cement of the apartment complex, one hand on my stomach, the other on my lips.

"See how her body's crumpled on that side?" Lily's flash exploded past my eyelids. "The ribs must've collapsed."

"On the first or second bounce?" I asked weakly.

Lily laughed as she circled the corpse. "You're catching on." She stepped between the girl's legs to focus on her face. The flash made perverse lightning.

"Do you ever rearrange things to make a better picture?" I asked.

"Only when I'm working with props, like car wrecks. I let the coroner move the bodies." She snapped the lens cap back on and returned the camera to its case. "Let's get out of here."

I was finally able to ask, "Who called, Lily? Wouldn't the cops...?"

"Don't panic, Sherry." She was already striding back to her car. "One of the guys from Richardson's party lives in the Towers. He found her when he chained up his bike and knew I'd be interested."

"Why didn't he call an ambulance or something?"

"Dead is dead, Sherry. If the police don't notify her family for an extra half an hour, what difference does it make? Her mom'll get a little more sleep before finding out that her baby couldn't hack it at the university. I'll tip the police anonymously before we get home. There's still a payphone at the Dennys."

Visions of Lily at work—lips parted, eyes focused in concentration, body perfectly encased in a tight leather racing jacket—chased me through the night. I finally gave up on sleep at 6 AM.

I wanted the bathroom, but I couldn't remember how the apartment was laid out. The first door I opened led to Lily's darkroom. The switch turned on a red bulb. Photographed eyes stared at me from every surface; some reflected her flash while others had clouded over. Lots of dead things: three kids who'd suffocated in a refrigerator echoed the pose of a gnarly old man who'd bled to death in a dumpster. There were little dead things, too, including a pile of viscera that reminded me of the toad I'd run over with the lawnmower last summer.

"Was last night an act?" Lily asked from over my shoulder.

The breath rushed from my lungs. Damn, I wished she'd stop creeping up on me.

I tore my gaze away from the photographs to face her. "What do you mean?"

Lily's eyes were a cold gray. I hadn't realized that before. "You're horrified by me and my art," she accused.

"No," I corrected, "I like it more than I'm comfortable with."

As I pulled her into the dark room, she closed the door behind herself and switched off the light.

When we'd caught our breath, I asked, "How do you find all your subjects?"

"I have a lot of people on the lookout for me. They call when they see something interesting." She pulled the string to switch the light on again. "Do you like one of these especially?"

I wanted to change the topic. I don't like people to know how I really feel; that's why I decided to study acting. When I was sure my voice was steady, I said, "That black-and-white one."

Cracks radiated across the windshield from a hole the size a head would make. Something dark pooled on the dashboard. Centered in the picture, floating on the dash, was a white card hand-lettered with "Happy 18th Birthday, Bill!"

Either the photographer had focused through the rear window, or she'd been in the back seat of the car.

"Take it." Lily pulled it from its clip. "I have the negative."

"Thank you." I held the picture by its edges as I padded naked into the bathroom.

After he let me into our apartment, Jacob stomped back into the bedroom. The lock clicked behind him.

A long shower did nothing to calm me, since I couldn't get clean clothes from the bedroom. I fixed a bowl of Cheerios and settled down with my laptop to read the morning news. The top of the screen featured the train accident. The story mentioned the annual midterm wave of suicides.

Returning to the front closet, I slid the print of Lily's photograph from inside my jacket. The windshield glass shimmered as if the sun had been very bright on the day of the accident. My gaze was drawn to the birthday card. I wondered if she had known Bill, if she used this photo to probe her own fascination with death. If it really was a memento mori.

Jacob's voice harped in the bedroom, carrying easily through the locked door. Whoever he'd brought home wasn't making him happy.

Then again, what did he have to be happy about? His relationship with me had deteriorated. His art school grades weren't good enough to score much of a post-grad appointment. He was a passable painter, not overwhelmingly original. His canvases had not been selected for Professor Richardson's private collection.

A midterm wave of suicides, I thought. In a certain light, Jacob's death would be a blessing, saving him from a lifetime of disappointment as a failed artist. Since Lily only photographed fatalities, maybe in the long run something Jacob did could actually be construed as art.

How to do it? A slip in the bathtub, head striking the tile?

Too much speed during one of his painting binges? Or she might like a spatter of crimson against our clawfoot tub. Whatever happened, the challenge would be to drive Jacob to deliver his own coup de grâce. How would Lily express her gratitude if I showed her something she'd never seen before?

I wondered when his guest might leave. I was eager to get started. I hoped I was actress enough to pull it off, even if I *was* only a junior.

With You by My Side
It Should Be Fine

Tolly adjusted the cracked mirror to catch the last of the daylight before he lined his eyes. Since the rats gnawed through the generator's insulation, he was forced to make up his face in natural light.

The bedroom door creaked open behind him as Doug emerged, on his way to check the solar oven on the roof. Tolly said nothing. He had learned it was better to leave the older man to his thoughts when he first emerged for the night. While Tolly had grown up on a diet of sun-crisped pigeon, Doug still craved the things he'd left behind. As if his dreams took him home, Doug missed the past most when he first got out of bed.

When Doug returned to the kitchen to carve up breakfast, the roast pigeon smelled amazing. Tolly's mouth watered. He arranged his low-cut blue dress to better display the hollow of his thin chest, then let the smell draw him into the kitchen. "I'm starved."

"It's kind of scrawny," Doug warned. "Rats got the other one before I checked the trap." He stripped the last of the meat from the bones with a scalpel.

Silently admiring the play of candlelight on the silver in Doug's hair, Tolly wolfed down his share of the pigeon and licked his fingers. "It's good." He brushed his cheek against Doug's shoulder. "I'm going out now."

"Good luck," the older man said.

Tolly wondered if he heard an accusation there. He knew he had to find a trick tonight; the cupboards were bare. He slipped on his pumps, then let himself out of the apartment and descended the three flights of stairs.

Broken glass and fallen tiles cluttered the apartment

building's lobby, slippery footing beneath his high heels. Tolly crossed the room cautiously. A broken ankle meant a long crawl up the stairs and nothing but pigeon to eat for longer. He craved applesauce. Better yet, he thought, canned fruit salad.

The door to the street held no panes. Tolly pushed the revolving metal frame around and stepped out, combing a hand through his long black hair. The street outside was deserted but not silent. A family of rats wrestled in the doorway across the street. Tolly ignored them and got moving. He never carried a weapon. Experience proved that he was not a fighter, that a gun or knife would only be turned against him. Shattered glass or rusty pipes were always underfoot if he needed protection from the rats.

Tolly followed Jefferson Street up to the river, then lounged against the graffiti-scrawled marble of Citizens Bank. A fire several blocks away reflected off the low clouds. Tolly watched the light show.

He worried about Doug. The older man had become even more withdrawn of late. It hurt Tolly that he could not be everything Doug needed. Recently, he couldn't even provide a decent meal for the two of them. That had to change soon, or Tolly would need to do something drastic.

Claws snicked against the pavement behind him, too heavy to be a rat. Tolly subtly noted the broken bottle at his feet before he turned toward the sound. Instead of an animal, he found a figure shrouded in a big black coat. Tolly leaned seductively against the cold marble and gestured toward the abandoned car where he conducted business.

"I'm looking for Tolly."

The feminine voice rocked Tolly more abruptly than anything she could have said. She pushed her hood back. Close-cut ashen hair accented her sharp cheekbones. Tolly couldn't remember the last time he saw a woman.

"I don't do women," Tolly said. "Try Fion or Dev."

She watched him closely. "Are you Tolly?"

"Yes, but don't waste my time. I have to get paid tonight, or Doug and I won't eat. Find Fion or Dev."

He walked away, but she kept pace. "Fion sent me here. I'll

pay you, Tolly, if you take me to Doug. It's very important." The woman drew a handful of something out of her coat pocket. She opened her fingers to reveal a rope of pearls.

Amused, Tolly wondered, "Where'd you get those?"

"From a friend."

"They're worth more to you, then. What would I do with pearls?"

She didn't withdraw her hand. "They're real."

"So are these." He fingered the large square emeralds at his ears. "I looted the jewelry store on the corner. So what? We can't eat jewelry."

She whistled shrilly. The clicking of animal footsteps returned. Tolly realized the woman had maneuvered him out of reach of the broken bottle. Fear knotted his stomach. He hated the thought of losing his favorite shoes if he ditched them to run.

A leggy black dog stepped around the corner of the bank. He crouched at his mistress's feet, eyeing Tolly with a toothy smile. "This is Onyx," she said. "Hold your hand out to him, palm down."

Shaking, Tolly did. Onyx nosed his fingers.

"He's yours." The woman's voice was tight enough that Tolly knew she was lying. Doug had told him about dogs. Tolly understood exactly what this strange pair wanted with the old man.

Tolly decided to play dumb and stalked past them. "I don't wanna eat your dog."

"Hang on." She strode after him. "What?"

"Usually I get paid with a can of vegetables. Spam, if someone's feeling generous. I even got sardines once." His heels snapped angrily against the pavement.

The woman halted in disbelief. "Sardines?"

Tolly ignored her and kept walking.

Shadows appeared ahead. Tolly glanced, unwisely, at the rubble at his feet for a weapon. As a warning not to pick anything up, someone flung a handful of pennies at him. The worthless coins stung his bare arms.

Behind him, Onyx growled. The woman whispered, "What's going on?"

Tolly faced a hard decision. Doug had drilled into his head that eventually someone would come to his rescue. Tolly knew that if he took the woman home, she would take Doug away. If he told the gang what she was, they would most certainly kill her, sooner or later. Doug would never have to know.

As Tolly struggled with the dilemma, the gang slunk closer. Tolly realized he couldn't ruin Doug's chance to escape. "Shut up and act male," Tolly whispered. "It's me they want. If you want to live, don't say anything."

A male voice mocked, "Who's that, Tolly?"

Tolly cocked one hip. "My trick. Leave him out of this. He doesn't see you and you don't see him, right?"

"What kind of animal is that?" someone else asked.

"That's his protection against being seen." Tolly sucked in a breath. "Can we get this over with? I'm hungry."

The men laughed.

Five, maybe six of them, Tolly estimated. He bit his lip, knowing he could still change his mind and betray the woman.

The men materialized from the shadows to rip away his blue silk dress. Their leader stepped forward. Drew was maybe twice Tolly's age, but something as terrible as the plague lurked in his olive-green eyes. He traced a finger along Tolly's collarbone. "You're getting thin."

Tolly admitted, "We've eaten a lot of pigeon lately."

Drew brushed the hair from Tolly's face and kissed him. "We'll make this worth your time, Tol."

Eventually, Drew held a flask to Tolly's lips. The shine burned some awareness back into his aching flesh. He swallowed greedily.

"You're a real gentleman, Tol," one of the gang taunted.

"Be nice," Drew hissed through bared teeth. "Tolly's been good to us. Pay him."

A canvas sack landed at Tolly's feet. He heard the cans clank inside it. Hunger made him lightheaded.

Drew kissed him again. "You're a good kid," he whispered. "Tell Doug to feed you better."

Tolly waited until Drew and his gang had faded back into the night before he knelt to open the sack. It contained a big can of beef stew, several cans of green beans—and one can of peaches. His mouth flooded.

"Are you okay?" the woman asked from behind him.

Tolly flinched. "I thought you'd left."

"I still need to find Doug." She shouldered out of her overcoat and wrapped it around Tolly's shoulders. "Why didn't you run?"

"What good would that have done? They know where I live." Tolly clutched the coat close, his fingers clumsy on the buttons. "They paid me," he said. "That's all that matters."

When he swayed on his heels, the woman caught him. His weight, slight as it was, sent them both to the pavement. Onyx crawled up beside them to lick Tolly's face.

Tolly smiled at the woman. "Thanks. You probably saved me from cracking my head open."

"Let's get you home." She helped him stand. Even though he wore heels, his head barely topped her shoulder. He shivered when she wrapped an arm around his waist.

"What's your name?" Tolly asked.

"Angie." She whistled for Onyx to stay close.

"You're here to take Doug home, aren't you? You're another time traveler."

She stiffened at his side, then forced herself to relax. "Doug told you about that?"

"When he found the cure for the plague, he expected someone to come after him." Tolly laughed quietly. "He'll bitch that it's taken you so long to come to his rescue."

Although they navigated the moonlit lobby with no trouble, Tolly faltered at the stairs. "Three flights up," he said.

"Isn't there an elevator?"

"Hasn't worked since we've lived here." He sank down onto the first step.

"I'll go get Doug to help."

"Would you?" Tolly was too exhausted to decide if she was lying again. He knew there was a better than even chance that she would just take Doug and go. It would be easier for Doug to leave if Tolly wasn't there to say goodbye. It didn't matter. This was the right thing to do for the man he loved.

Tolly nodded toward the left wall. "There's a flashlight under that newspaper."

Angie went to find it. "What's your apartment number?"

"You ask dumb questions." Tolly wiped at the eyeliner smeared below his eyes. "Third floor. It's the only place that's lived in. The trash in the hallway is pushed back from the door."

"You'll be okay?"

"Yeah." He took off one pump and weighed it in his hand. "The rats know I'll put this heel through their skulls if they come too close. Onyx should keep the wildlife away from you."

Angie shuddered. She whistled for the dog, then climbed the stairs.

Tolly's vision blurred. Angry, he squinted until the outlines of the rubble sharpened. He wished he didn't ache. Doug could give him something to make it better, if he wasn't leaving.

When Tolly woke on the davenport, Doug was staring out the picture window at the derelict city. The distant fire reflected from his sharp features.

"It's hard to believe our world came to this," Angie said.

"It happened faster than you would expect," Doug told her. "Losing two-thirds the world's population does that."

She didn't have an answer. "Your research notes will fit into a backpack, won't they?"

Doug gulped from the jar of shine in his hand. "And Tolly?"

"I'm sorry." Perhaps she was, but her voice held something ugly that Tolly didn't understand. "You'll have to leave him. Onyx can only travel with us two. It's probably best, anyway. He wouldn't fit in to your old life."

Tolly had heard enough. He swung his bare feet to the worn carpet and slipped into his bedroom. Tears burned his eyes, but he was too furious to let them fall. Why had Doug brought him home? Just to say goodbye? Why couldn't Tolly remember being carried in Doug's strong arms? Why did this have to be so hard?

Tolly was pulling a clean dress over his head when Doug tapped on the bedroom door. "You okay?"

"My shoulder hurts." Tolly wiped his face and straightened his spine, before he pulled the bedroom door open to face the older man. "You must have given me a shot. Thank you."

"Of course, Tolly. I—"

Tolly shook his head. "If you can save those people, go. I understand. Maybe you can save my parents this time." And then I won't need you so much, he finished silently. He walked back to the living room to rummage in Drew's bag of food, looking for the peaches. He vowed not to cry, not to make this hard for Doug.

Doug ducked into his own bedroom to pack up his notebooks.

Once Tolly had settled on the davenport, can and spoon in hand, Onyx rested his chin against his thigh. The dog gazed up with round, innocent eyes. Tolly stroked his head, marveling at the velvety softness of his ears.

Angie said, "Thank you for making this easy for Doug. You'll be happier here. No one in our society would understand…your relationship."

"Which relationship is that?" Tolly's voice took on an unfamiliar adult tone. "Doug took me in after the plague killed my parents. I was four. In return, I get food for us, however I can. But you're right: I wouldn't want to go anywhere they don't understand that we take care of each other."

"I thought you were…"

"Lovers?" Tolly supplied. "Doug doesn't like boys."

He pried open the can of peaches, spooned up one perfect golden crescent. He closed his eyes to savor its sweetness.

Against his knee, Onyx shivered, hackles up, staring at something that wasn't there. Tolly petted him, but the dog didn't respond.

"You were lying when you offered me Onyx," Tolly accused. "You need him to return."

"Yes." Angie sipped from her own jar of shine and had the discipline not to cough. "I felt I had to bribe you with something other than the pearls. Onyx was all I had."

As she examined the shine jar, Tolly noticed her long, lovely, unscarred fingers. He rubbed the white line that ran down his index finger and thought of other scars, unseen.

A shadow shifted behind Angie. Tolly watched Doug creep out of the bedroom, a needle glinting in his hand. Unobtrusively as he could, Tolly slid his fingers under Onyx's collar.

Doug jabbed the syringe into Angie's shoulder. Startled, she let go of her drinking jar. It bounced off the table's edge, spilling shine in a fan of liquid. Onyx lunged, but Tolly hauled him back, despite the leather collar cutting into his fingers.

As Doug dragged Angie to the davenport, he said, "Relax. I've given you a tranquilizer. It will keep you immobilized for two or three hours. I'm taking Tolly and your dog."

He turned her arm over and rolled up her sleeve. "This second shot is my vaccination for the flu. If it works, keep dressing like a man. Most of them can't tell the difference. There's a fortress of women holed up in Ontario. They'll shelter you."

Onyx wrenched loose and circled the davenport to lick Angie's face. Doug stroked the dog, but didn't try to grab him.

"What are you doing?" Tolly demanded. "You have to go back. People will die."

"They've been dead to me for years," Doug argued. Tolly knew people in the past sent Doug here after the first time travelers came back and confessed they'd infected the future with a plague. He had been supposed to study the disease, find a cure, and save the future. Then somebody ate his dog—and no one else came.

As if he'd followed Tolly's thoughts, Doug said, "No one ever came after me. It's been ten years, Angie. Where the hell have you been?"

The drug prevented her from answering. Tolly pulled Doug away from her and wrestled him into a hug, trying to soothe the older man's rising hysteria. "It's okay now," Tolly whispered. "You can go home now."

"No." Doug shuddered and stepped back out of his arms. Tolly stared hard at the floor, to keep the hurt out of his gaze.

"I won't leave you," Doug said.

Tolly frowned at him, confused and hoping so desperately that he hated himself for it. "Your people won't understand our relationship, she said."

"They wouldn't. We won't go back to them. We can go back to before Chenglei and Ichiko first came forward. We can keep them from spreading the plague. We can inoculate your parents. You could grow up with them, Tolly. You could go to school. Maybe you could…"

Tolly held up a hand. "Let's get out of here first."

Doug nodded. "Grab your jewelry box. We'll try to use the gems as money wherever we end up. And change into your exploring clothes. As Angie so tactlessly pointed out, the past was a different place."

Tolly went into his bedroom and lit the precious kerosene lantern. He removed his smeared makeup. Then he put on his daytime-exploring clothes: a ripped pair of blue jeans and a T-shirt that said Glass Spider Tour on the back. It was a good luck charm.

He looked slowly around his cluttered bedroom. The things he'd salvaged held memories, like the paintings he'd looted from other apartments, but most of his stuff was worthless. He pulled a couple of dresses from their hangers and rolled them into a ball that he put in the bottom of a torn backpack. He added his jewelry box, tucked in his best pair of pumps, and slipped in his sketchbook. The rest would have to stay.

When he returned from the bedroom, Doug frowned. "What all have you got jammed in there?"

Tolly shrugged. "I may have to work where we end up." He shouldered his pack, then picked up the forgotten sack of groceries.

Onyx whimpered at Angie, but heeled when Tolly tugged his collar.

Dawn bled into the lobby. Crossing the room was easier now. Tolly seldom did it in daylight.

In the street, Doug slid an arm around Tolly's shoulders. "Onyx's mind will move us when I trigger him. Hang on to me."

Always. Tolly wound his arm around the older man's waist and leaned his head against Doug's chest.

And then the future was different.

If you enjoyed this book, please consider leaving a review. Even a sentence or two—or something as simple as awarding stars—on Amazon, Barnes & Noble, Smashwords, or Goodreads will help other people find this book.

Not only do reviews help sell books, they inspire authors to continue writing. Thank you!

Story Notes & Content Warnings

I was ten the year my parents drove from Michigan to the Rocky Mountains for summer vacation. For me, the trip meant six weeks in the back of a truck camper: no TV, no radio. No parental supervision, since they rode in the cab of the truck. These were the days before handheld video games or laptop computers or even smart phones.

Mostly, my brother stared out the window and slept. Mostly, I read. I had a stack of books checked out from the public library back home. I'd just recently started reading adult novels. One of the first was *Dracula*.

There's a photograph of me sitting on a boulder outside the campground at Rocky Mountain National Park. It was beautiful there and I was excited about seeing mountains, but my dad and the truck were queued up in a very long line of campers and cars, waiting to see if there would be any campsites for the night. We weren't going anywhere for hours.

In the picture, I'm sitting on a boulder with a book on my lap. There might be a slight flush to my cheeks that has nothing to do with fresh air and sunshine.

My mom, who was a librarian, had a theory: everything I was too young for, I would misunderstand anyway. In the case of *Dracula*, she was wrong. Even if I didn't grasp the subtext, my world was rocked when Dracula drank Mina's blood, then sliced open a vein in his chest and fed her blood back—and she liked it.

Every horror story I write descends from that moment: when submission turned to pleasure, then to desire, then to hunger.

Here There Be Monsters

Early in 2010, Rain Graves invited me to be part of a writers retreat she was putting together in Northern California. She had been working at a mansion on the slope of Mount Tamalpais. She said the mansion was very haunted. Her plan was to gather a bunch of horror writers for four days of writing and ghost hunting. Before the weekend was over, Weston Ochse came up with the idea that we should publish an anthology of stories written at or inspired by our Haunted Mansion Retreat.

We repeated the adventure in the fall of 2012. I began writing "Here There Be Monsters" at that retreat. The story was inspired by a comment made by the mansion's caretaker, who wasn't afraid of ghosts in the house. The really terrifying things, he said, lived in the woods outside.

The mansion really has an abandoned swimming pool behind it, shadowed by redwood trees. I spent a very pleasant afternoon sitting beside the water, writing descriptions that appear in the story. Even as I enjoyed the peace and sunlight, I never stopped being aware that a mountain lion could be watching me through the trees.

"Here There Be Monsters" was written for *The Haunted Mansion Project: Year Two*, published by Damnation Press in 2013. Until I prepared to read at the book release party, I never considered how personal the story is or how much of my misspent youth it reveals.

CW: drug use, sex, violent death

In the Pines

This story was inspired by Nirvana playing Lead Belly's "Where Did You Sleep Last Night" on MTV Unplugged. The way Cobain's voice broke as he sang chilled my blood. In the years since I first heard the song, several girls have gone missing in Northern California. The news media is always relentless with those stories, dragging the parents on over and over to repeat the heart-wrenching details of the last time they saw their daughters. I tried to imagine what life would be like for the siblings of the missing.

"In the Pines" appeared in the Women in Horror issue of *The Sirens Call* ezine in February 2019.

CW: child abduction

The Acid That Dissolves Images

During one of my creative writing classes at the University of Michigan, an older man expounded on the gender differences inherent in storytelling. There were certain voices a woman could never master, topics she could never face, stories she could never tell. I was incensed. My imagination could take me anywhere and I wasn't afraid to confront anything. I still can't read the story without thinking, "Fuck you, buddy."

The impetus to use the quotations in the story came from Re/Search's edition of Octave Mirbeau's *The Torture Garden* and my husband Mason's love of French Decadent literature. When Medusa says, "Count your blessings; some people can't see," that quote was taken from the live Big Black album *Sound of Impact.*

The Octavio Paz quote from which I took the story's title comes from *Posdata.* According to Paz, "The acid that dissolves images" is criticism.

This story was originally published in *Lend the Eye a Terrible Aspect* from Automatism Press in March 1994. It was republished in the chapbook *Ashes & Rust* in October 2006.

CW: drug use, violence, suicide

Valentine

I've been writing about Alondra DeCourval for years. Her stories have appeared in the books *Fright Mare: Women Write Horror, Strange California,* and *Best New Horror #27,* in addition to many magazines.

One of the formative experiences of my life was when a friend's brother invited me to his university cadaver lab, where he taught gross anatomy. Thomas allowed me to hold a human heart in my hand.

I started this story with the image of Alondra holding Simon's heart in her hand. Of course, that morphed in the writing.

Simon Lebranche was inspired by my friend Brian Thomas's Renaissance Festival character, an immortal cavalier in too-tight

162

pants who traveled the world to fight for the underdogs, usually on history's losing side. Brian provided the battles Alondra lists in this story.

In addition, a trip Brian took to Oslo inspired the setting of this story. He brought me a brochure about Vigeland Park and the towering, monumental sculptures there. I knew I wanted Alondra to see them.

"Valentine" originally appeared on the *Wily Writers* podcast in September 2010. I listened through it for the first time at the original Haunted Mansion Writers Retreat. The story was republished in the chapbook *Alondra's Experiments* in February 2018. This is its first time in print.

CW: sex, bloody violence, attempted suicide

If you struggle with suicidal thoughts, please call the National Suicide Prevention Hotline at 1-800-273-8255.

The Arms Dealer's Daughter
In my *In the Wake of the Templars* novels, the main character Raena Zacari talks about being purchased as a bodyguard for Ariel Shaad, whose father owned a factory that made sidearms before the galactic war broke out. Once the novels were completed, Jeremy Lassen, my editor, encouraged me to write some short stories set in their universe. This is the only one I've published so far.

The story's influences date farther back. When I was a teen, my mom worked at a branch of the public library in Flint, Michigan. I'd go with her to work and check out all the books in the library's science fiction shelves. I discovered *Dangerous Visions* that way, which led to the works of Harlan Ellison and Philip K. Dick, and the short political fiction of Ursula LeGuin.

All those influences are visible in this story. In it are young people making questionable choices and acting out, all the while blind to the way their society works. There's a nod to *A Clockwork Orange*, too, and *Bright Lights, Big City*.

The story takes place amongst the multiplicity of creatures that inhabit the galaxy of my *Templar* books. That universe pays homage to the original *Star Wars* movie, where the Mos Eisley cantina scene hinted that humans were a minority in the galaxy.

This story is also flavored by repeated listening to Gary Numan's *Replicas* album, with its undercurrent of menace and the repeated appearance of electric friends.

"The Arms Dealer's Daughter" appeared as a bonus story in the ebook edition of *Space & Time* #133 in March 2019. The story has never before appeared in print.

CW: drug use, slavery

The Energizer Bunny at Home

This is the most autobiographical story I've ever written. In August 1994, my dear friend Jeff's first husband died in their bed after a short, horrific battle with AIDS. Blair was only 29. I poured my rage and grief at his suffering into this story.

In 1998, this story won the fiction contest at Death Equinox, the first convention I attended as a professional. The organizer offered me a reading slot, but I couldn't bring myself to say the words aloud.

When the story was republished almost ten years later, I got invited to read it at Pegasus Books in Berkeley, California. Reading the whole story aloud for the first time was hugely cathartic. After I finished, I realized that all the college students in the audience were too young to remember the AIDS epidemic. They'd never known a world without HIV. Thank science, testing positive is no longer automatically a death sentence. Jeff himself is still alive and kicking ass 26 years later.

"The Energizer Bunny at Home" was originally published in the *Death Equinox '98: Cyber-Psycho Convergence II* program book. The story was reprinted as "The Energizer Bunny Keeps Going and Going..." in *Instant City: A Literary Exploration of San Francisco* #4 (the Love issue) in Winter 2007.

CW: assisted suicide

Never Bargained for You

In 2012, my friend Dana Fredsti was working for Ravenous

Romance. She proposed an anthology of succubus/incubus stories, then contacted me. She'd read the original draft of the succubus novel I wrote with Brian Thomas—then called *As Above, So Below*—and told me I absolutely had to write a succubus story for her.

She was so enthusiastic that I got inspired to explore something that was a throwaway moment in the original novel. The succubus Lorelei and Ashleigh, the ghost who possesses her, sort through one of Lorelei's trunks of mementos. They stumble across a collection of laminated backstage passes. Lorelei muses about all the fun she had working in the music scene in Los Angeles. The scene got cut from the first half of *As Above, So Below* when it was published as *Lost Angels* in 2014, but appears in an altered form in the sequel, *Angelus Rose*.

When Dana wrote me back in 2012, I'd just finished reading the 33 1/3 book on *Led Zeppelin IV*, which explored the magical underpinnings of that album and Jimmy Page's scholarship into the occult. All the pieces of my story were there. I just had to put Lorelei in the right place at the right time: on the eve of Led Zeppelin's first US tour.

I watched *The Song Remains the Same*, read up on the Laurel Canyon music scene, and I've never had a short story come together so quickly.

"Never Bargained for You" appeared in *Demon Lovers: A Succubus and Incubus Anthology*, published by Ravenous Romance in January 2013.

CW: drinking, drug use, graphic sex, devil worship

Grandfather Carp's Dream
When I lived in Ann Arbor, I loved to escape to the Conservatory at the Matthaei Botanical Gardens. Especially when the snow flew outside, the Temperate House was toasty warm, filled with the scents of good clean earth and flowers.

My favorite part of the greenhouse was the carp pond, with its waterlilies. I'd take my notebook and sit at the edge of the pool, listening to the waterfall trickling down and watching the giant koi circle below. I wanted to honor the place by setting a story there.

Martha J. Allard asked if she could have a fairy tale for the anthology she was editing. I was grateful that she liked this one. "Grandfather Carp's Dream" appeared in *Out of the Green: Tales from Fairyland*, published by Urban Fey Press in November 2014.

Affamé

Many of my stories were written in a fury. Charlie Jane Anders has said, "Yoda was wrong. Anger doesn't have to lead to hate. Anger leads to everything good. Anger leads to tenderness, because it comes out of wanting to protect the things you love the most. Anger is the way into the story, and all the other feelings will follow." That was definitely the case with this story.

I was so tired of seeing young gay men demonized for their desires. I wanted to write the hottest vampire story that I could, without a drop of blood. I never thought I would see it published, but Dave Lindschmidt asked me if I had a story for *City Slab: Urban Tales of the Grotesque*. He accepted "Affamé" immediately. It was published in *City Slab* #10 in July 2007.

If you're curious, the title translates to "Famished."

CW: graphic sex

Mothflame

When we were in high school, my dear friend Martha J. Allard and I would down Diet Coke by the two-liter and lie on our stomachs on her parents' living room floor with our spiral-bound notebooks, listening to *The Midnight Special*. We spent years writing a novel we called *Crowd Control*. The characters spun out of David Bowie's *Ziggy Stardust and the Spiders from Mars*. We obsessively chronicled the rise and especially the fall of Ziggy, Asia, Weird, and Gilli. Time, distance, and misunderstandings temporarily separated Mart and me. The book languished, unfinished.

The summer I went to the Clarion Science Fiction Writers Workshop, I salvaged the scene where Ziggy flings wine bottles against a wall to demonstrate how distraught he is over his junkie boyfriend's death. "Mothflame" is the only thing I rescued from that unfinished novel.

Originally Chris was meant to be a genderless cipher on whom the other characters wrote their desires. In the end, she—like Medusa in "The Acid That Dissolves Images"—became the embodiment of their death wishes.

"Mothflame" was originally published in *Not One of Us #25* in March 2001. It was republished in the chapbook *Ashes & Rust* in October 2006.

CW: drug use, murder

Sound of Impact

In all of Los Angeles, the place I love the best is Griffith Observatory. I did get the opportunity to see Arcturus through its telescope once. The star was just as beautiful as I describe. The exhibits that the characters visit in this story were replaced when the museum was remodeled in 2006, but they were just as weird as they appear in this story.

The story's title comes from the live Big Black album from 1987. The album sleeve was printed with black box conversations between pilots and co-pilots—or pilots and air traffic controllers. In every case, the conversations end with the dispassionate phrase [Sound of Impact]. Reading them as a litany one after another made my blood turn cold.

"Sound of Impact" has only ever appeared in *Sins of the Sirens: Fourteen Tales of Dark Desire* published by Dark Arts Books in January 2008.

CW: bad sex, a dream of being in a crashing plane

Justice

I was still in high school when the guy I was dating took me to one of the two gay bars in Flint, Michigan. Pete came out to me by kissing a man there. We went back to the bar time and again. I was almost always the only girl there, which felt very liberating to me.

When originally conceived, "Justice" was my solution to the

tyranny of the gender dichotomy. Why, I wondered as I began this story, should the world be so divided by a facet of our bodies unseen by the world at large? Then, of course, I realized that even a gender-free utopia would have its personality conflicts. Someone bigger or more brutal would always try to enforce conformity. As tough as the surface I tried to project was, in those years of my own coming out, I was never under any illusion about my place in the food chain.

"Justice" was originally published in *Blood Rose* in April 2003. It was reprinted in the chapbook *Ashes & Rust* in October 2006.

CW: homophobia, violence, drug use

The Magic of Fire and Dawn

This was the first story I ever got paid for. Stories of mine had been published before this one, but this was the first time someone I didn't know liked my writing enough to pay me to publish it.

I'm still fascinated by the mythology of the Wild Hunt: faeries who howl through the woods at night to hunt down and punish good Christians who've wandered from home and hearth. There's a whole lot of influence from Terri Windling's Fairy Tale Series in this story.

"The Magic of Fire and Dawn" originally appeared in *Beyond Science Fiction and Fantasy* #18 in October 1990. It was reprinted in *Eternal Night* in August 2003.

Still Life with Shattered Glass

Several elements of this story were drawn from real life. The card on the dashboard beneath the head-sized hole in the windshield was something I saw in the newspaper after one of our high school football players died in a car accident. In reality, it was a graduation card on the dashboard. I was so horrified by the violation of taking—and printing—that photograph that I had to exorcize it by writing about it.

The girl who jumped from the University Towers apartment building died while I was going to school at the University of

Michigan. I never saw a photo of her, but as I wrote this, I was thinking of the photo of Evelyn McHale, the woman who jumped off the Empire State Building. I don't really know if there's a midterm wave of suicides at American universities, but it was rumored while I was in college.

This story has been accepted more than any other I've written, but the first two times it was accepted, it never made it to publication. Then it took third place in a story contest judged by *Cemetery Dance* magazine at the World Horror Convention in 2005. (Thanks so much to Kelly Laymon for strongly encouraging me to attend the award ceremony!) In addition to that cash prize, it was my first sale at a professional pay rate when it appeared in *Cemetery Dance* #54 in March 2006.

John Everson published the full-on erotic version, called "Still Life with Broken Glass," in *Sins of the Sirens: Fourteen Tales of Dark Desire*, published by Dark Arts Books in 2008. A third version, combining the first two, appeared in the book *Tales for the Camp Fire: An Anthology Benefiting Wildfire Relief,* published by Tomes & Coffee Press in 2019.

This current version combines elements of all of the previous versions in a way original to this collection.

CW: drinking, sex, suicide

With You by My Side It Should Be Fine
I wrote the initial draft of this story in the early 1980s. In 1986, it got me into the Clarion Science Fiction Writers Workshop. There it caught the eye of Algis Budrys, who made me believe for the first time that I could make a living as a writer. It also caught the scorn of Thomas Disch, who loved the story but predicted my gender based on my name and was highly disappointed when I wasn't a young man. He felt I didn't deserve to have written this story.

I'm not sure where I got the idea of the plague being carried forward into the future, but I remember lining up as a child in a school gym to get a flu shot during the first epidemic of my lifetime. AIDS was devouring men in New York and San Francisco when I was in high school. I guess I've been expecting the pandemic for a long time.

When I wrote this story, life beyond heterosexuality was barely acknowledged. It would be years before people understood what it meant to be enby. I like to think that Tolly discovered the word wherever he and Doug ended up, that he found himself reflected at last.

The title of the story comes from my absolute favorite David Bowie song, "Candidate." I love the album version, but I also love the goofy, over-the-top demo version. The emerald earrings that Tolly wears were another homage to *Diamond Dogs*.

"With You by My Side It Should Be Fine" is original to this collection.

CW: underage sex worker

Acknowledgments

Every book is written with the support of an unseen army, helping to hone each story until it's scalpel sharp. Each of these stories have been polished with the help of Mason Jones and Martha J. Allard.

Thank you to the teachers and members of Clarion '86, who pushed me to write these stories down. Thank you to Emerian Rich and the Quillz for their close readings of these stories. Thank you to all of the editors who've published these stories and made them better. Thank you to the Horror Writers Association for inspiring me to assemble this collection in the first place.

Thank you to L.S. Johnson, for her eagle eyes and thoughtful reading. Thank you to E.M. Markoff, for her ongoing emotional support.

Thank you to Eugenia, Kevin, and all the members of Shut Up & Write, Amy for the Sponsors Write-In, and Jenny for Writing Together, all of whom made space for me during the pandemic to assemble this book.

Thanks to the TBD Writers group, especially Jennifer Brozek and Alison J. McKenzie, for their encouragement. Thanks to Angel Leigh McCoy for all her help with my technical issues. Special thanks to Lisa Morton, for her example and inspiration and for her lovely introduction.

Finally, thank you to Brian Hodge, Meg Elison, J. Scott Coatsworth, and Thomas Roche for saying such very nice things about my work.

Other Books by Loren Rhoads

The In the Wake of the Templars trilogy:
The Dangerous Type
Kill By Numbers
No More Heroes

The As Above, So Below series, written with Brian Thomas:
Lost Angels
Angelus Rose

The Alondra chapbooks:
Alondra's Experiments
Alondra's Investigations
Alondra's Adventures

Nonfiction:
199 Cemeteries to See Before You Die
Wish You Were Here: Adventures in Cemetery Travel

To learn about new stories, works in progress, and exclusive offers like ARCs, sign up for Loren's monthly newsletter at the link at https://lorenrhoads.com/

Also Available from Automatism Press

Lost Angels – As Above, So Below: Book 1
by Loren Rhoads and Brian Thomas

In the days before the Flood, Azaziel was a Watcher, sent down to guide God's creatures on Earth. He fell in love with one of Cain's granddaughters and they passed her mortal life in bliss.

The succubus Lorelei doesn't know any of that when she sees Azaziel in her master's nightclub. All she knows is that the angel's fall will bring glory to Hell and acclaim to any succubus who accomplishes it.

Of course, Lorelei has no way to predict that Azaziel will try to tame her by possessing her with a mortal girl's soul. Can the succubus find an exorcist before the fury of Hell is unleashed?

9 781735 187600